"Leave me alone."

"I don't want to bug you. I want to understand. Why do you do it?"

I don't think he knew the answer. Neither did I.

"It helps me relax," he said. "I take a couple of swigs and the fear goes away. You know those eight goals? Every one of them I was feeling nice. Not bombed but nice. Every one. The one time I played sober, I got my teeth knocked out."

"It was a freak accident," I said. "Drinking doesn't help you score. You aren't relaxed now, either. Look at you."

"I'll have one more and I'll be fine."

SHEP GREENE was born in New York City and grew up in Connecticut. An avid hockey player, he also enjoys tennis, squash, and racquetball and is an accomplished skier and sailor. He lives in New York City.

ALSO AVAILABLE IN LAUREL-LEAF BOOKS:

TEX, *S. E. Hinton*
RUMBLE FISH, *S. E. Hinton*
TAMING THE STAR RUNNER, *S. E. Hinton*
RUNNING LOOSE, *Chris Crutcher*
THE CRAZY HORSE ELECTRIC GAME, *Chris Crutcher*
STOTAN!, *Chris Crutcher*
CHINESE HANDCUFFS, *Chris Crutcher*
THE CHOCOLATE WAR, *Robert Cormier*
JOHNNY VOODOO, *Dakota Lane*
FREE FALL, *Joyce Sweeney*

THE BOY WHO DRANK TOO MUCH

Shep Greene

Published by
Dell Laurel-Leaf
an imprint of
Random House Children's Books
a division of Random House, Inc.
1540 Broadway
New York, New York 10036

Visit us on the Web! www.randomhouse.com/teens

Educators and librarians, for a variety of teaching tools, visit us at www.randomhouse.com/teachers

ISBN: 0-440-90493-5

RL: 5.0

Reprinted by arrangement with The Viking Press

Printed in the United States of America

March 1980

30 29 28

OPM

This book is for my parents,
and for my daughters,
Schuyler and Thayer.

THE BOY WHO DRANK TOO MUCH

ONE

It was my mother who didn't want me to play hockey. My father didn't care; he played in high school and liked it, so it was okay with him. But my mother still didn't want me to play.

"I'm worried about your teeth," she said. "You have such nice, straight teeth."

"I'll wear a mouthpiece," I said. "Come on, Ma, please?"

"We didn't even have mouthpieces in my day, honey," Dad said to help me. "And I've still got that perfect smile."

He showed her. Secretly, I was hoping I would lose some teeth. Then I'd look like Bobby Clarke and have that same tough, undeniable look of determination. Being fifteen, I felt determined, but I didn't look it. Maybe no teeth would help.

"You don't even want to play hockey," my mother said. "You're just doing it because Art is."

"Come on, Ma, I've been playing hockey all my life."

"You've been skating on a pond with a hockey stick, you mean," she said. But she stopped arguing and put her hand on my cheek. "You have such a nice smile."

"I'll keep it that way, Ma," I told her. Before she could change her mind, I dialed Art's number and told him I'd meet him at the Sports Shop to buy some gloves and shin pads. As I put on my coat and went to the back door, I heard Dad trying to cheer her up.

"Maybe he'll get tired and drop out after a few weeks," he said.

That was back in November. It's February and I'm still on the team. I play center on our junior varsity third string, which gives me plenty of time to sit on the bench wondering when I'll score my first goal. I need a goal to get my letter. Art is playing defense on my line. He's my best friend. My oldest friend. We met in Cub Scouts when we were seven. Art got caught stealing the cookies and Mrs. Lipera sent him home. I thought it was cool to be thrown out of Cub Scouts so I walked home with him that day. We've been walking home together ever since.

Art's sure to get a letter. He's five five and one-sixty, and he's good at knocking people down. He just stands in front of the goal and throws his weight around. Me, I'm so light I have to skate my legs off just to stay alive out there. And I have to work much harder than Art does during practice. Improvement in this game comes very slow when you're a klutz like me, let me tell you.

One of the guys on our line, Buff Saunders, is just the opposite. He's a born skater. Comes from

Canada, where he started skating when he was four. Actually, he's too good for the third line. He's scored eight goals already this year, which is real good for a freshman, but Coach Anderson won't move him up. He says it's on account of his bad attitude.

"He's a troublemaker, a real wise guy," Art was saying. We were in the weight room next to the gym. Art rested the barbell on his chest and caught his breath. "Danny has math with him and says Mr. Wilkins sent him to detention seven times last semester. Among other things, he sleeps in class."

Art inhaled sharply and pumped the weights up and down. Six, seven, eight, nine times. Then he dropped the bar to the mat.

"So what?" I said. "Wilkins gives everybody detentions. What's that got to do with his ability as a hockey player?"

Art shrugged. "Besides," he said, "Buff isn't one of us. I wouldn't get too wrapped up with a guy like him." He bent over and took a few pounds of weight off the bar.

"What's that supposed to mean?"

"Well, what does he have in common with us?"

"He's on our team. And he's a good player. We could learn something from him." I was trying to convince Art with real practical reasons. But he wasn't buying.

"The only thing you'll learn from him is trouble," he said.

Sometimes, when Art is trying to convince me

of something, he gets a tone in his voice that I really resent. He sounds like he's a parent and I'm a kid.

"The guy's a liar," Art said. "A bald-faced liar. I'd stay away from him if I were you."

"Well, you're not me," I said. "And what makes you think he's a liar? Any more than anyone else is."

"He told Danny he can drive," Art said smugly.

"Maybe he can. He knows a lot about trucks."

"And he told Danny he *owns* a car. A 1960 Thunderbird."

I didn't know if it was true or not. It didn't sound true. Old Thunderbirds are pretty rare and very expensive.

"So?" I said, trying to sound unbothered.

Art snorted.

"When Danny asked him to see it, Buff told him he couldn't just then. He said it was in the shop getting fixed."

I didn't know what to say. Art stared at me, resting the weights on his shoulder without saying a word. It wasn't worth arguing with him. He already had his mind made up. And I didn't have much to work with.

"Come on," I said. "Cut the blabber and give me the weights. You're done."

"Sure thing," he said.

He shoved the barbell at me.

I put it on my shoulder and took some deep breaths to get started. Art counted while I worked. After three or four presses the sweat started to come and I knew I would be very tired when I finished.

Hockey took a lot of time. It was eleven-thirty now, which meant we still had three hours of classes, two hours of practice, and a whole night of studying before the day was done. That's a long day. Every once in a while my parents asked me if it wasn't too long. My grades were holding OK so far, and my hockey was improving. But my father wanted my grades to improve, too. Grades come first in our family, so my parents didn't really appreciate all the work I was putting into my hockey.

Art understood how important the hockey was, since he's my best friend. So it was that much harder for me to figure out why he didn't like Buff. Hell, neither one of us knew him better than to say how're you doing. But Art really didn't like him. There were bad vibes or something between them. Me, I kind of liked the guy. During practices he looked out for kids who weren't as good as he was. Gave us tips and stuff. None of the other good players paid us any attention. I figured, coming from Canada and all, he was probably lonely and wanted to make friends. But he was an outsider. Why no one wanted to let him in I don't know. Maybe Art knew something I didn't.

After the presses I did some knee bends with the weights, then some sit-ups and push-ups without them. Art put some more weight on, but before he could get started, Mrs. Watson came in and told us to clear out.

Mrs. Watson was one of the girls' gym coaches. She was the nicest and youngest one, too. Last fall the PTA raised a big stink when she suggested that the girls should be allowed to use the boys' athletic facilities. A news crew from WKBW came down to school and put her on television. The PTA chairman resigned. The whole thing seemed a little ridiculous to me, but some people had strong feelings about it, one way or the other. After the storm died down, the girls got permission to use the weight room. Now a bunch of swimmers, the gymnasts, and the track and field teams use it.

Regardless of how you feel about girls playing sports, you've got to admit they look pretty good when they do. Art and I like to wait around as long as possible. After you've been working hard for twenty minutes or so, your muscles are sticking out, your chest is full, and you tend to speak with a deeper voice. Art also tends to laugh a lot.

We were watching the girls without letting them see us when Mrs. Watson spotted us and told us to scram.

"Ho, ho, ho," Art said. "Be out in just a second." He picked up his towel and started for the door.

"You left your watch," Mrs. Watson said.

"Ho, ho, ho, so I did," Art said. "Ho, ho, ho. Thanks, Mrs. Watson. Ho, ho, ho."

"Now go, Arthur." She smiled. "And take that one with you." She pointed at me and smiled again. "How's the hockey going, anyway?"

"It's coming along," Art said. He jerked his

thumb at me. "We're still waiting for him to score, though."

"Well, don't push it," she told me. "Just keep thinking and trying your best. You'll score."

"OK. Thanks for the advice." We said goodbye and turned to go, when *bam!* I was on the mat. A girl with blond hair was standing over me. She was out of breath. So was I.

"I'm very sorry. I didn't see you. I'm sorry I'm late, Mrs. Watson."

"That's all right, Julie," Mrs. Watson said. "But you should watch where you're going."

This Julie character bent over me and offered a hand. I refused it, naturally. Art helped me up. She wasn't a big girl—I was a full head taller. But she did seem to be in pretty good shape. She must have been moving pretty fast when she hit me. "I didn't see you," she said again. "Are you all right?"

"Of course," I said. In truth, I felt slightly dazed and wanted to get out of there. Everyone was staring at us.

Mrs. Watson clapped her hands. "OK. Swimmers over on the isometrics. Susan, Allison, and you three, start on the barbells. The rest of you pair off and get going on sit-ups. Forty of them."

There was a collective moan, but everyone went about their business. "I'm really sorry," Julie said again. Then she lay down on the mat and started her sit-ups.

"That's all right," I said. "I'll live."

"Come on," Art said. "We're going to be late." He grabbed me by the arm and steered me out the door. We didn't have time to shower, and the science lab was so hot that everyone in the class was kidding me about my B.O. by the end of the period. My chest hurt from where Julie had hit me, too. It was turning out to be, as my mother always said, one of those days when I should have stayed in bed.

When I got to our usual table in the lunchroom, Tina was there with Art. Tina is Art's girl friend. She has a good body and a nice smile. Art told me that's why he likes her. But as far as I can tell, they haven't gone to bed with each other. Art wants to, but she won't. She says they're both too young. So Art says that until she grows up, he'll just kiss her and nothing more. He doesn't want to pressure her. That sounds like a good approach to me, but I'll bet they have some interesting conversations when they make out.

Tina is mad at Art right now because he gave her a hickey the size of a quarter four nights ago and it still hasn't gone away. "I'm running out of clean turtlenecks," she was saying as I sat down and started to eat. "My mother keeps asking me why I don't wear a blouse and sweater for variety and I have to make up an excuse. It's so *embarrassing*!"

"What do you tell her?" I said. She sure didn't seem embarrassed.

"That all the other kids are wearing them," she said with a shrug.

"They are," Art said, "because they've all got hickeys to hide." Impulsively he grabbed Tina and pulled down the neck of her turtle. The hickey was still there, bright as a birthmark. She gave a shriek of self-satisfaction, and Art tried to give her another one. But Tina pushed him away.

"You've got a hickey to hide. You've got a hickey to hide. You've got a hickey to hide and I don't care!"

Everybody around us laughed, then quieted down quickly as Mr. Sawyer cruised by. Checking on things. After he passed, Tina hissed at Art, "You'd smile on the other side of your face if my father found out."

As Art was about to answer, Buff Saunders came over. Carrying his tray. "Hi," he said. "Mind if I join you?"

Nobody answered. He wasn't part of our group. Nobody but me and Art knew him.

"Sure," I said when no one else would. I poked Art in the ribs to make him move over to give Buff room on the bench.

Buff sat down next to me. I was nervous. He picked up his fork and started to eat. I tried to get a conversation going when no one said anything.

"You ready for the Bridgeport game?" I said when he finished his first mouthful of food. He nodded.

"It'll be a tough one, John Murphy says," he said. John Murphy is the team captain. He should know. Buff licked his lips nervously when nobody said anything. "Bridgeport has big players," he said. "And they like to fight, I hear."

"Don't believe everything you hear, Saunders," Art said. "I know every guy on the team. Grew up with half of them. They're not so big. If they want to fight, we'll fight."

Buff could feel that Art didn't like him. He moved closer to me and stared at his food. "They look pretty big to me," he said softly.

"Oh, I hope you don't get hurt," Tina said to Art suddenly. "I couldn't stand it." She seized Art's hand in hers, but he pulled away from her.

"Knock it off, Tina," he said. "I'll be OK. It's those two you ought to worry about." Meaning Buff and me. "If you guys are going to play hockey, you better learn to defend yourself. Fast." He gave a little laugh.

"I don't like to fight," Buff said.

It was a funny thing for him to say. We all looked at him. He was big, very mature-looking. He had dark brown hair, and you could tell he was already shaving. Every day. He looked much older than he was. He could pass for eighteen or nineteen in the right light if you didn't look too closely at him. But if you looked him right in the eyes, you knew he wasn't eighteen. Buff had the eyes of a little kid. You know the look I mean—big, round, and wet-looking. As though he was about to cry.

Tina laughed. "You can't be a very good hockey

player if you don't fight," she said. "Isn't that right, Art?"

Art nodded. Art had this theory about hockey. You try to scare the other team right from the start. Check them and make them worry so much they can't concentrate on their game. He calls it his Intimidation Strategy and says it's the way the pros play. From what I've seen on TV, I agree with him. But I don't think that way when I play. I think skill's more important. And Buff is one of the few guys on our team who's got skill. But he wasn't defending himself in front of Tina. So I did.

"Buff's better than Art or me," I told her. "He's already scored eight goals this season." Her eyes went wide and she looked at Art, who nodded. "He learned to skate in Canada when he was four." Buff shied away from Tina in embarrassment. I knew if he didn't say something to these people, he'd never get a second chance. "Go on," I told him. "Tell her about Canada."

"Do they fight during hockey games in Canada?" Tina was teasing him, but he didn't catch it.

"Sure," he said. "Some guys do. They'll hit anything that moves on the ice. I don't like playing that way. Someone might get hurt."

"It's not supposed to be a picnic out there, Saunders," Art said. He'd been waiting for a chance to jump on Buff.

"You and my father would like each other a

lot," Buff said, and looked at Tina. "Dad was a real good player. He liked to fight, too. But I'd rather win by stick-handling past four guys to score."

"It's much more fun to watch," Tina said. "It can be very graceful sometimes."

The two of them stared at each other for a moment, realizing that they felt the same way. Then the bell rang and the lunch period was over. We picked up our trays.

"I've got an idea," Tina said. "You guys will be tired after the game on Saturday. So why don't you come on over to my house? We can just hang out."

"I don't want to sit around after a game," Art said. "Let's you and me go to a movie."

"With your father driving us again? Ugh. Besides, my parents will be away. We could have a good time."

"We could double with John Rogers and Sissy," he said.

"A party would be more fun," Tina decided. She nodded at Buff and me. "You two should bring dates."

"I think it's a stupid idea," Art said.

"But, Artie, we could play some records and dance," she said.

"I don't think you should have people in while your parents are away," he said. "Your father will hit the roof."

"It'll be just the three of you and your dates," she said reasonably. "Records and pizza. I'll talk to Daddy. He won't mind." She patted Art on the hand and turned to Buff. "Now," she said, "who are you going to invite?" Obviously she already had somebody in mind.

"I'll have to think about it," Buff said. But the look on his face said there weren't many candidates for the job.

"Do you have somebody special you'd like to bring?" she asked.

Art rolled his eyes.

Buff shook his head. "Not really."

"Then I'll fix you up."

"Who're you going to set him up with?" Art said.

Tina stood and picked up her tray. "Someone who just adores hockey players," she said. "Especially good ones."

"Who is it?" Art picked up his tray and followed her. "Rita Harris? Brownie Thompson?"

"Never mind," Tina said. "It's my surprise. See you at my house at seven-thirty, Buff. And don't get into too many fights in the game on Saturday."

They both laughed. "I won't," Buff said.

"See you," she said.

Art walked off with her. We could see he was still trying to find out who Tina had in mind for Buff's date.

"She's nice," Buff said.

"Yeah," I said. "They've been dating each other since seventh grade."

Buff said something else about Tina, but I wasn't paying much attention. I was already thinking about how I was going to find a date by Saturday night. And what I was going to say to her once I found her. I decided the search could wait until after the game on Saturday.

TWO

We play most of our games at Crystal Rink. It doubles as a wrestling arena when the weather gets warm. Locker room gossip says that the owner of the rink, Bruno Walters, was a hockey great in Canada as a kid. He came to the United States wanting to build the finest hockey emporium in North America. I don't know what happened, but instead he built Crystal.

The boards are full of splinters, the ceiling is so low that high-flying pucks knock out the lights, and some section of the bleachers collapses during every game. My parents stopped coming after the third game. I thought my mother couldn't take the strain of watching me play. But I found out later they stopped coming because a panel of roofing tin fell one night and landed ten feet from them. Nobody got hurt, but from then on they listened to the games on the radio—at home.

The one nice thing about Crystal is that it is small. So you don't notice how few fans show up to watch you get creamed in a game like the one with Bridgeport. And I was getting creamed, even though we were winning, 2–0. Every time I went into the corners to get the puck, one of their defensemen came after me. His elbows felt like raw potatoes hitting me in the head and chest. I was tired and couldn't fight back. Art was tired, too, so he couldn't help much. I held on to the boards to keep from falling down and tried to freeze the puck, trapping it with my feet to stop play so the referee would blow his whistle for a face-off. But the defenseman kept beating me on the back with his elbows and I started to fall.

All of a sudden I was free and the crowd was cheering. I looked around, and there was the defenseman spread out flat on his back on the ice. Buff had the puck pinned against the boards. When the ref blew his whistle, Buff swept the puck over to him and skated to me.

"What happened?" I said. Meaning the defenseman, who was just getting up.

"You looked like you needed a little help," Buff said. "So I gave him a check. Maybe next time he'll think twice about elbowing you."

It must have been a pretty good check to make the crowd cheer like that. The defenseman kept looking over at Buff and me as he skated to his bench to take a rest. I felt better already, knowing he wouldn't be picking on me. I grinned at Buff as we skated to the face-off circle when the referee motioned us into position.

On the face-off I swept the puck back behind me. Art was there and sent it forward up along the boards. Perfectly. The puck bounced off the boards, and I picked it up and passed it to Buff on the left side. He stick-handled his way around one player and worked his way out of our zone, across center ice, and passed back to me. Perfectly. The crowd started to yell louder, so I looked toward their goal. Only one defenseman against two of us. We had a chance to score.

I passed back to Buff as we crossed their blue line and skated like hell toward the net when he wound up to shoot. But Buff missed the puck. It wobbled weakly toward the defenseman. He gathered it on the tip of his stick as Buff charged toward him and flipped it back with a sharp snap of his wrist. I knew his pass would be a high one. I turned back up ice but lost sight of the puck. In the lights somewhere, I thought. But it never landed.

Something was wrong. The crowd stopped yelling. I looked back toward their goal. Everybody was skating toward center ice. Some guys had their gloves off—a fight, I figured.

But it wasn't a fight. When the referee got things straightened out, Buff was huddled on all fours. There was blood everywhere. Guys were saying things like "Give him room!", "Let him breathe!", "He got it in the nuts!", and stuff. Then Buff looked up.

His mouth was a mess—blood and spit, swollen twice the size. He had tears in his eyes and was trying to spit but couldn't. All his front teeth were gone, lying on the ice somewhere, probably not far from the puck. When he realized it was me, he tried to smile.

"Look, Ma," he said. "No cavities!" And he started to cry. I grabbed him by the shoulders to keep him from falling.

"You've got to get off the ice, Buff," I said. "Can you skate or do you want a lift?"

He nodded. A bunch of us skated him to the bench. Patsy, the trainer, took one look and called for an ambulance. We were at the hospital in fifteen minutes.

"Don't leave me," Buff said. He stared up at me and Patsy from the stretcher.

"We'll be right here," Patsy said. "Give me your number. I'll tell your family where you are, what's happened to you."

Buff shook his head. "He's not home yet." It was hard to understand him.

"Who?" I asked.

"My father. He works late tonight."

"What about your mother? We'll call your mother."

"I don't have one."

Patsy looked at me. I barely knew Buff, much less that he didn't have a mother. But now didn't seem to be the best time to get better acquainted.

"Will you stay with me?" he asked. "Make sure I get home all right?"

"Sure," I said. "I'll wait for you." Then he was gone, wheeled by a guy in a white jacket through two doors.

Patsy went back to the game. He said to call if

there was a problem. I sat down to wait. I was still wearing my hockey gear.

Hospitals look nice. They're clean and bright looking and they smell good to me. But I remember being in one for a back operation. I was there only a week, but it felt like a year. A very painful year. Ever since then, whenever I go into one, I feel uneasy. I can't sit still or keep my mind on the magazine article I'm reading.

After waiting for an hour, I got up and paced. They were probably finished with Buff's teeth by now, I thought, but they must have found something else to fix—an arm or a leg, maybe. Not being a patient person, I didn't wait for the doctors to come tell me what was going on. I went to look for them. I followed the same path Buff's stretcher took through the double doors and down the corridor.

In case you're wondering, nobody seems to notice a kid in a hockey uniform in a hospital. I poked my head in and out of some examining rooms, which were empty, and called Buff's name once or twice before I found him. The door said, "Examining Room 7."

Buff was lying face up on an examining table. His eyes were closed and his lips were swollen black-and-blue. A great face for a horror movie. When I sat down, he opened his eyes.

"What did they do to you?" I said.

Buff mumbled. He could barely open his mouth.

When a kid in a hockey uniform stalks down the corridors of an emergency room at a hospital, yelling for a doctor, people notice. The noise flushed a covey of nurses from the check-in desk. They flew down the hallway toward me, followed by an intern who went right in to Buff and started to work. A nurse cleaned Buff's mouth as carefully as she could, while the intern got his sewing needle and thread and a hypodermic needle. It was a painkiller, but it didn't look like enough to me.

"In the pros they don't even use painkillers," the intern said. "The shock to the surrounding tissues temporarily knocks out the pain receptors, so they just grab a needle and thread and . . . away they sew."

He was in no hurry, though. He was very careful with Buff. He told him what he was going to do before he did it, that it would hurt a little when he put the hypo in his lips, and that he was also going to have to stitch up his gums.

I watched the whole thing without throwing up. Buff stared at the ceiling and cried. Because of the pain, I thought at the time. But later Buff told me he never even felt the needle.

THREE

The hospital was in the crummy part of town. When we got outside, Buff told me he lived five minutes away. So we walked. On the way he told me the anesthetic was wearing off but it didn't hurt too much. He could talk fine. I wanted to know more about his mother, but we talked about sports and school instead. Buff wasn't doing well in school, especially math. He wanted to drop out.

"In four months I'll be sixteen," he said. "I could just drop out. Nobody could tell me what to do. I could get a job."

"What would you do?"

"I could drive a semi," he said. "You know, those huge twin-axle trailer trucks?" He started shifting gears as we climbed the hill. "I could drive all over the States and live in my truck."

"Don't you have to be eighteen to get a license?" I said. "You need a special license."

"I'd lie about my age."

What Buff was saying sounded stupid to me. Very stupid. He was making me feel uneasy. What he wanted was so different from what I wanted—or what my parents wanted for me. Suddenly he was a complete stranger to me. I really didn't know him at all, I told myself. And I didn't know this part of town, either. So I felt very uncomfortable, walking through the bad part of town at night in a red, white, and blue hockey uniform with a guy I hardly knew. I wanted to be a good guy, to be responsible and help him out. He had been nice to me. So I really had to walk him home. But after that he was on his own.

Just as I had that thought, he threw his arm around my shoulder. "We could do it together," he said. "You and me. We could sign on a big rig and haul potatoes from Maine to Florida. Or roll cattle from Vancouver to Montreal."

I laughed and shook myself free. "Come on, Buff. Be serious. I can't even drive a car yet."

"Then you can work the CB radio and I'll drive. We could do it. Good friends can do anything."

"Please," I said. "I never kiss on the first date."

"I really appreciate what you've done for me," Buff said. "It's the kind of thing only a friend would do. A good one."

"Sure. But you've just had twelve stitches in your mouth, Buff. You've got to get home. And I've got to get home."

"We're here"—he turned around and swept his arm in the direction of his front door—"414 South Graham, Apartment 2B."

Once upon a time 414 South Graham had been a nice place, a big old house with high ceilings and hardwood floors. A comfortable house for a big family. Now, with a rusted-out washing machine in the front yard, it was a dump. I didn't know what to say. Buff must have read my mind.

"Come on up. You can call your parents to come get you."

We entered through a side door and climbed a flight of stairs lit by one bulb. It dangled at the end of a kinky cord. There were smells in the hall that I didn't like, but Buff didn't seem to notice. But he did notice the coughs and moans coming from the half-closed door on the landing.

"That's old Mrs. McClennon. She's always sick," he whispered. We crossed the landing to another door. Buff ran his fingers along the molding until he found the key.

Buff's apartment was big, with lots of windows. It made the furniture look small. A couch and three chairs with dirty cushions were arranged around the television set. The fireplace was boarded up. Next to it was a big iron bucket with magazines and newspapers in it.

"The telephone's next to the couch," Buff said. While I was on the phone, he flipped on the TV set and pulled off his pads and jersey while he watched cartoons. I listened to the phone ring and looked at him. With no shirt on, and the light of the set shining on his face, he looked very tired. And very sad. The way my father looks sometimes when his business is going crummy. Buff's lips were swollen, and the ends of his stitches stuck out from his face like little black whiskers.

There was no answer. I hung up and took off my shin guards, thinking about Buff's eight goals. I wanted to ask him if he'd mind giving me one so I could get my letter.

"Why do you play hockey, Buff?" I asked instead.

"My dad wants me to play in the pros," he said, without taking his eyes away from the TV.

"Do you want to play professional hockey?"

"Nope. But my dad wants me to awfully bad."

"You're a pretty good player. If you worked at it, maybe you could get a college scholarship."

Buff frowned and changed channels. "My dad was a Junior League player in Toronto," he said. "Any ability I have comes straight from him. I don't have the build for professional hockey, not even for good college hockey. And besides, this thing changes everything."

When he said "this thing," he meant his mouth, his accident. Looking at it again, I decided that no matter how bad I wanted to be popular and attractive to girls, I did not want to look like Bobby Clarke. Or Buff Saunders.

It must have been very painful for him. But he didn't let on. He changed the channel. Then he got up and went into the kitchen. "Do you want some food?" he said.

"Let me try my parents once more," I said. I did, but there was still no answer. So I decided to stay for dinner.

Buff seemed pleased. He bustled around the kitchen, buttering bread and heating a can of stew for us. I could have eaten the whole thing myself, but I concentrated on splitting the portions equally. When I put the empty pot in the sink, Buff looked at me.

"What are you doing?" he said, meaning the pot.

"I was going to wash it out."

"You didn't leave any for my dad," he said.

"Oh. I didn't know," I said. I carried the pot back to the stove and scooped stew from our plates. "How much should I leave?"

"Here, I'll do it," he said.

When Buff put the plate in front of me, I could see why he didn't think he had the build for college hockey. He was starving himself to death. One cube of meat, three slices of carrot, one-quarter potato. The breakfast of underdogs. I ate it in three bites. Small ones. I wanted to say something, but in one of those rare moments of tact I decided to keep my mouth shut. I knew Buff was hungry. That meant either his father had some odd ideas about the adolescent diet or they couldn't afford more.

I tried my parents again.

"What does your father do so late?" I asked as I listened to the phone ring.

Buff turned down the volume. "Right now he runs the Hobble Hill Tavern."

"No kidding? That's a nice place."

"Yeah. I hope I get to eat there sometime. Before he gets fired. My dad always gets fired sooner or later."

"Why?"

"Because someone always has it in for him."

"How do you mean?"

"Someone always tries to blame him for something he didn't do. Like stealing money for food or something."

Then Buff got up and picked up his plate. We were on our way out to the kitchen when we heard the front door slam. "That's him," Buff said. He quickly gathered up his stuff.

"I'll be right back," he said. He disappeared into the back of the apartment, leaving me alone in the kitchen. I walked into the living room to meet Buff's father.

Mr. Saunders' key rattled in the lock. He swore softly, jiggled the door handle, and entered.

"Who you?" he said.

He was a stocky man, overweight, with a red face and scraggly black hair. I introduced myself and told him about the accident. He didn't seem very upset.

"What's he look like?" Mr. Saunders said.

"He's lost four teeth and he's got twelve stitches. He's black-and-blue all over."

"I didn't lose mine until I was eighteen," he said.

"It must have hurt," I said.

"Hurt, shmurt. The pain goes away."

He tugged at his upper front teeth, the two big ones. They came out in his hand on a piece of silver wire. "When he heals a little, Doc Clark will make him one of these."

Mr. Saunders snapped his teeth back into place, threw his jacket on the couch, and went into the kitchen. He pulled an orange juice container out of the refrigerator and poured. I thought it was water. But he put an olive in it. When he lifted his glass to take a swallow, something behind me caught his eye.

"Wow," he said. "Did you get it but good."

Buff was standing right behind me. Hair combed, clean white shirt. Mr. Saunders broke into a big grin. And when Buff opened his mouth, Mr. Saunders laughed with delight.

"You keep this up," he said, "and you won't have a tooth in your head by the time you're eighteen. Let me look at you in the light."

Buff followed him into the living room. His father sat down on the couch and tilted the light so he could see better. He inspected Buff's mouth the way a vet checks a horse's teeth, peeling back the lips to show the gums. Buff winced once or twice, but he didn't say one word. When Mr. Saunders was done, he slapped Buff on the back.

"Hell, you'll be fine. Did you score?"

"We were just into the second period, Dad."

"Well, you know what I say—you got to score early. Get a leg up on them. Keep the pressure on."

"They're the best team in the league, Mr. Saunders," I put in.

"All the more reason to get on the board first. Then keep them on the boards." He meant we should get on the scoreboard first and then check them hard to keep them from organizing their game plan. He kicked off his shoes. "What's for dinner?"

"Stew," Buff said.

"Lots of it," I said.

"Bring it. You a wing?" he said to me.

"Center."

"Who's the other wing?"

"Dennis Jones," I said.

"Jones? Any relationship to Cassie Jones? Played for Toronto in the Fifties?"

"His father owns the Sunoco station," I said.

"No kidding. I thought he was still in Montreal."

I started to laugh, but Mr. Saunders groaned and rubbed his eyes. He poured another drink and told Buff to hurry with the stew. For a moment I thought he acted like he was beginning to get drunk. But when he put down his glass, he laughed. He sat back on the couch and threw his head back and called so Buff could hear him from the kitchen.

"The chef quit today," he said. "Four times before lunch. The city health people found mouse droppings in the pantry and told him to wash down the entire floor. When the kitchen boys were finishing up, they knocked over fifty pounds of fresh shrimp for this evening's seafood special. We had to reprint the menu for this evening."

"What happened to the shrimp?" I asked. Buff brought out the stew and put it in front of his father. Mr. Saunders started to eat. Watching him and listening to a conversation about fifty pounds of shrimp made my stomach growl. "Did you throw it out?"

"State law says we can't serve it like that," Mr. Saunders said. But he winked. "Of course, there's a nice shrimp salad on the luncheon buffet tomorrow. Fifty pounds of it."

Buff nodded. "Just a hint of linoleum in the sauce, though."

We all laughed. Mr. Saunders poured another martini. Buff looked over at me and gestured silently that I ought to try my parents again. My father answered the phone and it took some time to get everything straightened out with him. When I hung up, Buff and Mr. Saunders were arguing.

"I'm not going back! I don't like it and I don't want to play!" Buff shouted.

Mr. Saunders slammed his hand on the coffee table and got up. "No," he yelled. "You can't quit like that! I won't let you quit! I never did and you never will! A Saunders never quits!"

"Stop! Stop!" Buff said, waving his hands in front of his face as though he was clearing a cloud of heavy cigar smoke. Neither of them seemed to notice me in the doorway.

"Don't tell me to stop!" Mr. Saunders roared.

He lurched forward and tried to grab Buff by the back of the neck. But he tripped over the coffee table. Buff twisted away, anger flooding his face. He didn't even notice that the collar of his shirt was ripped.

"Don't touch me or I'll kick your brains in!" he screamed.

Mr. Saunders took a half-step of surprise, almost a stagger. He looked over at me and then at Buff. I wished I could have disappeared.

"What did you say to me?" Mr. Saunders said.

Buff was panting. He looked scared and angry at the same time. He kept knotting his fists, looking from his father to me and back again, as though he was trying to decide whether to run or fight. He couldn't do either, but he also wouldn't back down.

"I said if you ever try to hit me again, I'll make you wish you never had," he said.

"I wasn't going to hit you, Buff," Mr. Saunders said very calmly.

"You would have if *he* wasn't here. You're so drunk you almost forgot."

I prayed silently that Buff would shut up. Mr. Saunders put down his glass and looked from me to Buff again. I think he was wondering whether I would help Buff if they fought.

"I'm not drunk, Buff. See?" he said. And he walked a three-foot straight line. "And I'm not going to hit you. But I am your father and I'm due a little respect."

"I demand respect, too."

"You've got it. But you will not stop playing hockey," Mr. Saunders said. "We've been through this before."

"Right!" Buff shouted. "And you were going to stop drinking. Remember?"

He was heating up again. He looked around for more fuel and saw the martini glass.

"Put that glass down!" Mr. Saunders said.

Buff ignored him. He took a sip and imitated his father's movements to taunt him. He swayed back and forth, using his free hand to gesture as he spoke.

"When the kitchen boys were finishing up," he slurred, "they knocked over fifty poundsh-sh of fresh-sh sh-sh-shrimp."

When Buff looked at me and laughed, I couldn't help grinning. He was pretty good.

"Stop that!" Mr. Saunders said.

"Why should I?"

"Because I'm not drunk!"

"Yes, you are! You're stinking drunk!"

For a moment I thought Mr. Saunders was going to drop the subject by telling me to get out and Buff to go to bed or something. That's what my father does when he gets so angry he can't talk. But Mr. Saunders was different. He looked at me and gave me a crooked little smile, as though he was embarrassed. I smiled back at him, wanting to say something to make him feel better.

But then Buff took another sip of the martini. And Mr. Saunders lost his temper. Everything happened in a second. He straightened up and blinked his eyes. Then he took one very quick step forward, caught Buff by the neck with his left hand, and pinned him against the wall. The martini glass shattered on the floor as Mr. Saunders drew back to hit Buff. When I realized he was aiming for Buff's face, I started to yell.

FOUR

"Well, what happened then?" Ruth said.

I was sitting in her kitchen, telling her about Buff's injury, the game, and his father. Her full name is Ruth Benedict, she's forty-eight, and she lives alone. But she likes company like me and she also needs odd jobs done—jobs that pay well but don't take too long.

Ruth used to be married to a guy named Tommy and has had a hard life, she tells me. But she sure does laugh a lot. I like her because even though she's as old as my mother, I can always talk to her.

"Mr. Saunders belted him in the mouth," I told her.

"With his fist?"

"No, he slapped him across the side of the head. Like this." When I showed her, she winced.

"Wow, it must have hurt with all those stitches," she said. She peeked at the potatoes she was boiling and then looked at me again.

"Who is this Buff character, anyway?" she said. "You never mentioned him before. Is he new in town?"

"He's lived here for almost a year. I didn't know him at all before I joined the hockey team. We play on the same line, but he's a much better player than I am."

She nodded at me to keep talking while she set up her mixer.

"He's better than Art, too. He's already scored eight goals."

"Wow!"

"Yeah! Eight. And I haven't even scored one. I'll never score."

"When I played softball a hundred years ago, I never got a hit unless I reminded myself I was doing it for fun," Ruth said.

"Well, right now I can't say I'm exactly having fun. The coach keeps screaming at you to go out there and win. And your parents argue that hockey is not an 'appropriate activity.'"

"What qualifies as an appropriate activity?"

"Getting good grades. How boring."

"Well, they're doing it to help you. In the long run, good grades probably help you more than a team letter."

They probably do. That wasn't the point. I grabbed a knife and chopped up some of the potato peelings on the cutting board. Ruth stood at the stove, one hand on her hip and the other poking a fork into the chunks of boiling potatoes. Waiting for them to get soft enough to mash. I was thinking about Mr. Saunders.

"Why do people get drunk?" I said.

Ruth frowned. "Lots of reasons."

"How do you act when you're drunk?"

"I don't drink," she said.

She pushed back a puff of loose hair. "Some people act funny, though. They laugh and shout, and kiss and hug everybody. Other people get nasty. Or sad. Or crazy."

She turned the heat off and drained the potatoes.

"My Tommy used to sing sad songs when he was drunk," she said.

"My father puts on old records and sings along. Did you ever hear one called 'Shoot the Sherbert to Me, Herbert'?"

"No, but I'd like to."

"I can see how you can get drunk having a good time," I said. "But lots of people I know don't seem to have a good time. So why do they do it?"

"There's a lot of money in this town," Ruth said. "And where there's money, there're also problems."

"What kind of problems?"

"All kinds. Jobs, marriages, money, kids, parents. You name it. Getting drunk is one way of coping with problems. It's not a very good way, though. Hey, get off your duff and help me."

I carried the pot from the sink to the mixer while Ruth plugged it in. When she got it going, I fed it chunks of potato and she added the milk and butter.

"Do you know someone who has a drinking problem?" she asked over the whine of the mixer.

"No," I said, thinking about Mr. Saunders again.

"At least, I'm not sure." Maybe Art was right, maybe Buff was too much of a wise guy. If I'd been that way with my father, maybe he would've hit me, too. Even if I did have stitches.

But all of a sudden Ruth shut off the mixer and stared at me. "Do you have a drinking problem?" She looked so upset I had to laugh. Me with a drinking problem?

"No. Of course not."

"You promise you'd tell me if you did?"

"I promise."

Ruth relaxed a little and started the mixer again. "You're getting to that age," she said, "when life will ask you more questions than you can possibly answer and make more demands on you than you can possibly meet. So you'll need help. Don't be afraid to ask me for help."

"I won't be," I said.

She smiled at me as she scooped the mashed potatoes into a serving dish. Then she hustled the dish into the oven to warm and slid the dirty pot into the sink, all in one smooth move. It was nice that she was so concerned about me. Ruth was a good friend. She worried about me. I wanted to call her by her first name, but I could never bring myself to do it. Instead I told her that Tina had canceled her party.

"How come?"

"Because Buff got hurt. And because I forgot to get a date."

"Forgot? You didn't forget."

"Yes, I did. Anyway, it's rescheduled for next

weekend. Tina has fixed Buff up with a date. Someone who really likes hockey players."

"It sounds like fun," Ruth said. "If I didn't have so many gray hairs I'd join you. I'd like to meet this Buff Saunders."

"Maybe I'll bring him by and introduce you."

"Maybe you will. But when you say maybe, it usually means probably not."

"We'll see," I said. And grabbed a fingerful of mashed potatoes from the dirty pot in the sink as I headed for the door. Ruth used twice as much butter in her mashed potatoes as my mother did.

"Good night," she said. "Please come again."

"Good night, Mrs. Benedict," I said. "I will."

On my way home I thought about her offer to help with any problems I had. Not that I have any problems that you or anyone else doesn't have at one time or another. But it's nice to know someone is there to back you up when you need it.

Maybe that's why I keep thinking about Buff. He doesn't have anyone I can see to back him up. He's all alone. And life isn't going so hot for him right now. He's got problems. I can tell by looking at his eyes. So I'm concerned about him.

Part of it has to do with him being new to Chicopee. In this town people have known each other for a long time, the way Art and I have. We've become a habit with each other. When somebody new comes in, it takes time for him to work into the situation.

The other part of it is that Buff *is* different. He comes from Canada, so he sounds different. Not a lot, but still. And he has no mother. I've never known anyone my age who didn't have a mother. Maybe that's why his eyes are so sad and why he needs a friend so much.

All I know is I was getting creamed out there and he helped me out. When you're on the wimpy side, it's nice to have friends like Buff. They can make life much more enjoyable.

FIVE

I never did get a date for Tina's party. Art kept reminding me I was missing a golden opportunity. He meant that Tina's parents were going to the Virgin Islands for their vacation and we would be alone. Make-out city.

"The Virgin Islands, for Pete's sake," he kept saying to me.

He had to whisper because we were sitting in my living room using the phone. My mother was sewing at the dining-room table. Every time the machine stopped, we had to whisper.

"Call someone, anyone," he hissed. "We may never get another opportunity like this until we're twenty-one."

He shoved the phone at me.

"Dial," he ordered.

"I could call Harriet Rooney," I said.

"Harriet Rooney? She's got the body of a two-year-old."

Art took the phone away from me and made me look him in the eye. "You have a chance to score, dummy. Do you understand what I'm saying? You, a man, can have sex with the woman of your choice this Saturday night. So you might as well pick one with knockers."

"Knockers are for doors," I said.

I'm no dummy. I know about sexual intercourse. But I'm not going to get worked up about it the way Art does. Life is already complicated enough. Sex would only make it more confusing for me. He says he knows what he wants and it's Tina. He spends a lot of time thinking about her and working on her. Not that she's letting him get any that I can see. And I was pretty sure he wouldn't get any on Saturday, even if Tina's parents *were* in the Virgin Islands.

"OK, OK", Art said. "Call Hot Harriet Rooney."

I did but she wasn't home. It was too much for Art. He decided to go to the pharmacy for some aftershave.

"If you don't show up at Tina's with a date," he said as he put on his coat, "then it means you're a fag."

I didn't want to be called a fag. So I worked pretty hard to find a date. Harriet couldn't go—she had to baby-sit. And Beth and Andrea wouldn't go, not with me on such short notice. There's a proper way to invite a girl out, apparently—a way I haven't quite figured out yet. But what's the big deal, anyway? If you can call up a guy for a movie at the last minute, why can't you do it with a girl? Or why can't she call you? Sometimes I wish I had an older sister. But only sometimes.

Anyway, I decided I wouldn't go. I'd be a fifth wheel. Then I remembered that Buff would expect me there. I was the only one who knew everyone. I had to go. Maybe I could sneak out when the lights got low.

Art wasn't kidding. When I got there, he started calling me "Sweetie" in front of everyone else in the playroom. Buff hadn't arrived yet, but his date was there. She had her back to me and was looking through Tina's record collection, which was sizable. Albums lay in careless heaps around the stereo. As I took off my coat, Tina introduced me.

"I'd like you to meet Julie Seidman," she said.

When the girl turned around, I recognized her immediately. She was the one in the weight room. The one who had knocked me down.

"They've met," Art said in a high-pitched voice. He pointed at Julie with a limp wrist. "She's the brute who ran into him in the gymnasium. The nasty thing."

Julie didn't get the joke, which was just as well.

"I hope you're all right," she said. "I can be so clumsy."

"No permanent damage," I said. "I should have watched where I was going."

"And I should have been more careful."

She smiled so nicely it took me a couple of glances to realize she was wearing a retainer. She acted as though she didn't even have one. Right away I figured Buff would have a good time with her. Anybody would.

"Tina tells me you're on the hockey team," she said. "I'm on the track team myself."

"No kidding?"

I was grinning like an idiot. As though I'd never met a girl jock before. But I couldn't tell whether her eyes were gray or green. She was waiting for me to say something more, and I was trying to think of something.

"How about that?" I finally said.

It was the best I could do. We looked silently at each other, while she wondered why I was grinning so dumbly. Then Tina walked up to us. She was very firm.

"Julie is *Buff's* date," she said, glaring at me as if it was my fault he was late.

I looked at my watch and tried to think of a good excuse.

"Don't worry about me," Julie said to Tina. "I'm sure he'll get here."

"It's just that I like my parties to be boy-girl boy-girl," Tina said, taking Julie's arm. "We still have a couple of dips to make. Will you two excuse us?"

When she and Julie went to the kitchen, Art punched me in the arm.

"Did you see those muscles?" he said.

"Julie's? No, I didn't notice."

"They ripple," he said.

He drew up his sleeve and flexed. "Just like these."

Art has good muscles. And he knows it.

"Where?" I said. "I can't see a thing."

Art unbuttoned his shirt and slipped out of the sleeves. He flexed again, one pectoral, then the other.

"Hey, stop that!" I said loud enough so the girls could hear. "You want to get arrested for indecent exposure?"

"Hey, Tina!" Art yelled. "Look! My nipples are winking at you!"

The girls peered over the counter which separated the kitchen from the playroom. Tina had seen it before. Many times. She went back to work.

"Hey, Julie!" Art laughed. "Can you do this?"

He winked his nipples at her. Julie looked down quickly and busied herself with Tina. Art laughed louder.

"Hey, Julie! You can feel my muscles if I can feel yours. All of them."

Julie gave no reaction. I could see she wasn't too pleased. Sometimes Art doesn't know when to stop.

"Come on," I said. "The show's over. Get dressed before you catch the sniffles."

Art buttoned his shirt, took a handful of potato chips, and sat down.

"Where's your Canuck friend?" he said.

"Don't call him that."

"Which? Canuck or friend?"

"Either. You sound like a snob."

Art sighed a phony sigh. "Where—oh—where can Buff Saunders be?"

"I don't know. I'm not responsible for his behavior."

"You should know where your friends are."

"I helped him home from the hospital, that's all."

"You may think that's all you did, but he doesn't. He thinks you two are bosom buddies," Art said. "The way he watches out for you on the ice, you'd think he was your older brother. Or your boyfriend."

I ignored that. "He did what any teammate would do. Any good teammate, that is."

Art looked up and smiled as Tina and Julie came to the table with more food. "Speaking of teammates," he said to Tina, "how's my tight end doing?" They kissed, ending our conversation, which was fine by me.

Buff showed up an hour late. He had a whole case of beer with him. He put it on the floor in the playroom.

"I had to go to three different places to get it," he said. "Nobody would believe my driver's license." He pulled out his wallet. "It's my dad's old Canadian one. I held my thumb over the corner, where the birthdate is," he said. "I tried three supermarkets, but everyone spotted it. Then I tried a corner store. We got to talking about hockey, the guy who ran it and me, so I told him a little story about me growing up in Canada and playing for the Boston Bruins."

"You did *what*?" Tina said.

Buff took out a beer and twisted off the cap.

With no front teeth, he really did look like a professional hockey player. Even Art was impressed.

"I never even had to show him my card. He asked me how he could help me and I told him. It was that simple."

"That's a pretty neat trick," Art said. "Looks like he short-changed you on the case, though."

There were three empty slots in the case.

"I had a couple on the way over to limber up," he said.

Art helped himself to a bottle. "It's good beer," he said after he took a sip. "Remember your parent's party?" he said, looking at me. "With the keg?"

Last summer my parents had a Labor Day picnic down by the river behind our house. They bought a keg of beer and more food than a supermarket for all their friends. By the end of the day all the food was gone, but there was plenty of beer left. Art stayed over that night and the two of us snuck down to the keg for refills. We were watching a horror flick on TV. It was the first time I ever got smashed. Art, too.

"I can see you guys are old pros," Buff said. "Later on we can make boilermakers. Beer gets a little boring after a while."

"Well, nobody better go and throw up on Mother's couch," Tina said gaily. "If you have to barf, go in the garage."

We all laughed. Buff hoisted the case onto his shoulder and carried it to the garage. He brought one six-pack to the table.

"Put your empties in the box," he said.

Art put a record on and came back to the table, snapping his fingers. He finished his beer, put the empty in the box, and opened another one.

"Fifteen left," he said. "That's three apiece."

"The store closes at ten," Buff said. "If you think we're going to run out, I'll go get some more."

"I can't drink more than one or two," Tina said. "I'll get bloated."

"How about you, Julie?" I said. She hadn't touched her bottle. And she hadn't said two words to Buff. He didn't give her the time of day. He was talking to Tina, making her laugh.

"It tastes pretty bitter the first couple of sips," I told her.

"Oh, I like beer." She smiled. "I have one every Sunday with my parents at lunch." Then she sat forward and tucked her hair behind her ears. "But I'm in training," she said, "for an AAU regional meet in June. I do the two-hundred-meter run."

"That's four months from now," I said. "If you're worried about what one beer will do to your chances of winning, then maybe you should have at least three or four. Relax a little."

When she laughed, her hair flew out from behind her ears again. Her hair was sandy-colored, straight and cut in bangs. The kind of hair style that's easy to take care of. She had nice skin. No zits. And her eyes were green, I decided. With maybe a little gray in them. She didn't even wear lipstick or eye shadow. No artificial anything. And in a way, I thought that was very sexy.

She took a sip of her beer and frowned.

"Do you think Tina would mind if I got a glass? I don't like drinking it from a bottle."

Tina and Buff were still talking, so I decided not to bother them. Art was reading the back of a record album. I took Julie to the kitchen and found her a glass. When she poured the beer into it, the muscles in her forearm twitched.

"Why does a runner lift weights?" I said.

"The same reason a hockey player does. To get in shape."

"But you don't need to use your arms. I do."

"It's all part of the discipline."

"Sometimes Art goes a little too far," I said.

Julie backed up against the counter and put her glass down.

"It happens all the time," she said with a wry smile. "I don't mind."

She tucked her hair back behind her ears again and took a sip of beer.

"Some boys aren't used to seeing girls compete. It makes them nervous. But girls can be just as bad. They say *very* unkind things."

"Like what?"

"Personal things. Sexual things."

I didn't want to be nosy.

"It must be tough," I said.

"I'm a little sensitive about it," Julie said. "There's no reason to be, actually. If you don't have a big bosom, then they start saying you're not really a girl. To them, you can't be a girl if you compete. So you have to prove it to them. You've got to be real careful about how you dress. Don't wear jeans all the time or they call you a dike."

I laughed. Julie rolled her eyes at the ceiling.

"As though a skirt makes you a real woman," she said. "But that's why I put this one on." She motioned to her skirt. "So nobody would talk about me behind my back."

"I spotted you right away," I said. "In spite of the muscles and short hair. The clothes give you away. Only a real girl would wear a color-coordinated skirt and blouse."

We laughed together, and Julie tucked her hair back behind her ears. Looking at her, I figured it must be pretty important to her to compete in track. Otherwise, why put up with the criticism? She made me think about me and hockey.

"How'd you get into track?" I asked.

Julie shrugged and her hair flew out from behind her ears again. I liked it better that way.

"I always liked running," she said. "I want to be very good at something."

Just then Tina came in. She was very excited and probably a little drunk. I was starting to feel pretty good myself.

"You've got to see what Buff can do," she said. "Come on in here." And she dragged me by the hand into the playroom. Buff was sitting on the couch with Art.

"Show him what you showed me," Tina told him. "The thing with your teeth."

Buff smiled up at me. I could see the hole where his front teeth had been. "I don't know what you're talking about, Tina," he said with a smile. Then he put his hand to his mouth.

"It's disgusting," Tina said. "Go on, show him."

"It's ridiculous," Art said.

"What is?" I said.

Buff took his hand away and smiled at me again. The hole was gone. There were four teeth there. Buff had gotten his bridge.

"They're like the stars," he said. "They come out at night."

He bent over and spat them into his hand. Tina squealed with delight. Art looked like he had seen it all before. Julie cracked up.

"Unbelievable," I said.

Buff sucked his upper teeth back into his mouth, pushed them around with his tongue, and fitted them back into place. Then his lower teeth.

"I think I like them better out," Tina said as she watched him. So he spat them out. "What's it like to kiss with no teeth?" she asked him.

"Wanna find out?" he said with a laugh.

Art got up from the sofa and grabbed Tina. "Come on, let's dance," he said.

Tina looked wordlessly at Buff but stepped out into the middle of the room with Art. Buff sucked his teeth back into his mouth as we watched them start to dance.

"Watch out or you'll choke on them," I told

Buff. He was really showing off. He put his teeth back in and took another beer. Julie and I watched him drink half of it. Then he reached in his back pocket and pulled out a brown bottle. Whiskey. He poured it into the beer bottle until it was full again. Then he put the whiskey back in his hip pocket.

"Ever had a boilermaker before?" he said to me. "They'll really knock you on your ass."

I refused the bottle when he offered it to me. So did Julie. She looked at Art and Tina dancing instead. You could tell Art was getting drunk. He was losing his coordination. After he almost fell down twice, he decided to take a break and let Tina dance by herself. He came over to Julie and me to get a beer.

"Tina's on automatic pilot," he said, breathing hard. Then he sidled closer to me and whispered in my ear. "Virgin Islands, baby. Give her more beer to really soften her up and then make my move." He took a sip of beer and nodded at me.

One thing about Tina on a dance floor, she has no shame—she gets out there and goes crazy. Frankly speaking, whenever she starts dancing I realize how much more mature she is than I. Sexually, I mean. Especially when she's drinking.

When Julie saw how Tina danced, she turned to me with a look of astonishment on her face.

"Tina is a very expressive dancer," she said. "She uses her body very well."

"We went to Miss Hollywell's Dancing School together," I said.

"And Miss Hollywell taught her *that*?" Julie gave Miss Hollywell a deep nod of respect.

Art took a sip of his beer for added strength. Then he rocked back and forth on his heels, picking up the beat and rhythm so he could launch himself back into the dance without missing a beat. But just as he was about to take off, Buff cut in. Tina smiled at him and threw her arms around his neck. They danced away from Art, Julie, and me. Art started to swear and sat down in a funk.

Julie and I watched Buff and Tina dance together. He may have come from Canada, but he danced like an American.

"I'm going to dance," Julie said. She bent over and undid her shoelaces.

"What're you doing?"

"Taking my shoes off. It's easier that way."

I took my shoes off. And before I knew it, we were slipping and sliding around the room like a pair of dust mops. People say I'm an energetic dancer. That means I have more moves than skill, that I have a good time out there even though I don't look very good. It's true. Julie wasn't much better. She danced like a runner, plugging away dependably at a nice even pace. As we danced, I wondered what it would be like to kiss her. So I tried to think of something more important. Like scoring a goal and getting my letter. I discovered that the movements involved in making a slap shot fit in very nicely with the beat of the music.

"What do you call that step?" Julie asked.

"It's a new dance," I said, stealing the puck from her and skating up ice. I showed her how, and she caught on right away. "It's called the Hockey Hustle."

Art jumped up from the couch. "The Hockey Hustle? How do you do it?"

"Like this," Julie said, showing him. "But you can't do it in shoes."

"No way," I said. "No shoes allowed on the ice."

Art took his boots off and caught on after a couple of tries. The three of us did the Hockey Hustle from one end of the playroom to the other. Art fell down twice. He laughed like a crazy man the first time. As I helped him up the second time, he was muttering.

"Who tripped me?" he said. He was getting pretty drunk.

"Denis Potvin," I said, picking the name of his favorite defenseman.

"Denis wouldn't do that," he said, leaning on me for a moment. "Why would he do that?"

"You'd gotten by him and were about to score," I said. "It was the only way he could stop you."

"Did he go to the penalty box for tripping me?"

"No, the referee never called it. Denis was too smart."

I could see Art was getting tired. He was breathing hard and kept blinking his eyes, as though he was trying to stay awake. And he wasn't thinking too well, either. But I felt great. The music was loud and I wanted to get back to dance with Julie.

"He's the best player of the game," Art said. He smiled to himself and shook his head with admiration as he leaned on me. I was hoping he would sit down.

"Bobby Clarke is better," I heard Buff say behind us.

Art and I turned around. Buff had been listening to us. He took a sip of beer and kept his eyes on Art, looking for his reaction. Or a fight—I wasn't sure which. I didn't want to find out, either. I took Art by the arm and tried to make him sit down.

"Denis Potvin is the best defensive player of the game," I said. "Bobby Clarke is the best offensive player."

When I pulled on Art's arm again, he wouldn't budge.

"Bobby Clarke is the dirtiest player in hockey," he said, edging closer to Buff. "And he's a grandstand player."

"You don't know bushwah," Buff said.

When Art pushed up against Buff, almost spilling his beer, I grabbed Art's shoulder. Julie stepped back. She didn't want to get caught in the middle.

"Look," she said, "if you two guys want to debate the finer points of hockey, why don't you go do it somewhere else and let the rest of us dance?"

She looked at me, hoping I would support her. But I was a little confused. She was supposed to be dancing with Buff. And Tina was supposed to be dancing with Art. I wasn't even supposed to be here now. Somehow everything had gotten all switched around. Art must have been thinking the same thing I was. He blinked at Julie.

"I thought you were with *him*," he told Julie, poking a finger at Buff.

"Don't do that," Buff said, pushing Art back.

There was a brief shoving match. I got involved, grabbing Art around the waist, while Julie and Tina backed Buff into the corner. When everything got straightened out, Tina stepped into the middle of the room.

"Things have gotten a little out of control," she said slowly, looking from Art to Buff. "If you two can't be civilized, then you'll have to leave. Right now."

Her face was flushed with excitement. I wasn't sure whether she was going to cry or laugh. But she sounded as though she meant what she said.

"I'm civilized," Art said.

"I'm civilized, too," Buff said. He sounded surprised that Tina was criticizing him as well.

"Then I suggest you continue your discussion someplace else and let these two dance." Tina nodded at Julie and me.

I took Julie in my arms and we started to waltz. Away from Art and Buff. Art turned to Tina.

"He said Denis Potvin is a jerk," Art said.

"I did not," Buff said.

"Did, too," Art said.

"We *don't* want to hear it." Tina closed her eyes and clenched her fists. Art looked concerned and huddled around her, trying to make her open her eyes. Buff leaned over.

"I said he wasn't the best player in hockey," he said.

Then he stalked to the garage door, flung it open, and disappeared. Tina flopped into a chair. Art tried to apologize. But Tina wouldn't hear of it.

"You bore me," she said.

Art stomped to the garage door, slamming it behind him. There was silence in the playroom for a moment. Then Julie squeezed my hand. I looked at her and she smiled.

"You can relax now," she said.

The muscles in the small of her back were strong and hard. I wanted to leave my hand there, maybe even a little lower, but it didn't feel completely natural. So I remembered what Miss Hollywell taught me and placed my hand on her side. Below her ribs, lightly. She smiled at me again, and I started thinking about her lips.

The first time I ever kissed a girl we were underwater. Chickie Adams and I were swimming in the river behind our house. We were ten or eleven, and we both had our eyes open. I liked it. But before I could find out if she liked it and wanted to do it some more, she moved to California. I made up my mind that the next time I kissed a girl and liked it, I'd ask her right away if she liked it. Not that Julie was falling all over herself to kiss me. She wasn't. Maybe she didn't even like me. But when the record ended, she did put her arm around my shoulder and lean against me. And my hand finally felt comfortable on the small of her back as we waited for the next record to drop down.

"You two seem to be having a good time." Tina smiled at us. "Almost as good as the one I *was* having."

"Buff's a good dancer," Julie said.

"Good isn't the word," Tina said. There was a horrible crash in the garage. Then silence. The doorknob turned and Art walked into the playroom. His hair was messed up, his shirt was ripped, and he was breathing hard. "Somebody oughta teach him how to fight clean," Art said. "And hold his liquor."

We raced into the garage. "Careful," Julie said. "There's broken glass everywhere." When Art and Buff were fighting, they must have knocked over some empty bottles—or thrown them at each other. One of the doors to the driveway was open. Tina turned on the outside light. We found Buff on his knees in the snow next to the garage. He was still throwing up. Each time he did, his whole body jerked as though someone was punching him in the stomach.

"Do you think he's all right?" Julie asked.

"Maybe we should make some coffee," Tina said.

"Yes," I said. "Make some coffee. But first you two help Buff in while I check on Art."

"I hope he hasn't thrown up all over my mother's couch," Tina said. She followed me inside.

We found Art dozing off in a chair. Tina looked at him for a moment and then recoiled with a horrible expression on her face. She started to scream and Art opened his eyes. "What's going on?" he said. "What's the problem?"

The problem was a pool of blood spreading around his right foot. He was so drunk he didn't even feel it.

SIX

Art went to the doctor's the next day and came back with a cast on his foot. He called me up and I went over to his house to talk about it. Mr. and Mrs. Collins asked me a bunch of questions, but we stuck to our story, which was that Art stepped on the bottle in the dark when he was taking the garbage out at Tina's house. I don't think they believed it, but they didn't press it. They were more concerned about Art. He was taking it pretty hard.

"I'm out for the rest of the season," he told me. And stared at the cast on his leg. When Art had stepped on the bottle, he'd almost completely severed a tendon. So his doctor put a cast on it to keep his foot from moving and damaging it more.

"How long do you have to wear it?" I asked as I signed my autograph.

"The doc will take a look in eight weeks."

"That puts us into April—you'll be back in time for the play-offs."

"The doc says it won't be fully healed for months."

I'd made up my mind before I got to Art's house that I wasn't going to feel guilty about his bad luck. If Art hadn't gotten so drunk, this wouldn't have happened. I wasn't going to take the blame for him not playing hockey. No way.

"Think on the bright side," I said, trying to cheer him up. "Now you have enough time to do all those things you've been wanting to do."

"Like what?"

"Like pulling up your English grade. And getting more attention from Tina."

Art glared at me. Suddenly I realized I had stuck my foot in my mouth. And he wasn't going to let me take it out. So I kept putting it further in.

"You know what I mean," I said. "You can get Tina to take care of you—carry your books and stuff. She likes the nurse bit. And while the rest of us are getting beat up on the ice, you and she can play doctor. You can give each other examinations."

I thought I was being pretty clever. Witty and sociable in a difficult situation. Which tells you how little I understood Art's feelings.

"Did anyone ever tell you that you sound like a horse's ass?" he said.

"No. Why?"

"Why? What are you, an idiot?"

I was pretty sure I wasn't. But I didn't answer, just to be safe. I couldn't figure out what he was driving at.

"I'm not going to see Tina any more," he said. "I've called it off."

You could have flattened me with a feather. One thing I knew about Art, he really liked Tina.

"I'm sorry," I said. "I'm really sorry."

His eyes were watering. "You should be," he said. "If he hadn't been at the party, none of this ever would have happened."

Art hobbled to the bed, threw himself down, and buried his face in the pillows so he could talk without looking at me. Otherwise, he'd start crying.

"I never should have listened to you," he said in a muffled voice. "I should have stayed a million miles away from both of you. He's bad news to begin with. I hate his guts."

Art lost control and started to bawl. I sat down next to him to let him know that I wasn't going to walk out on him and that he could cry as long as he wanted. I know I would have. After a while I patted his shoulder and got him to stop.

"Come on," I said, "come on. You're going to shrink your bedspread."

But Art didn't laugh. Instead, he rolled over on his back and glared at me. His eyes were red and his nose was running.

"Get out of here," he said.

"I'm sorry," I said. "I was just trying to get you to laugh. To cheer you up."

"You caused all this," he said. "You and that damned friend of yours."

"You're my friend, too. My best friend. I wouldn't hurt you."

Art's lips drew into a grim, straight line. He wiped his nose on the back of his arm.

"Then prove it."

"How?"

"Stop messing around with Saunders."

"Why? What have you got against him?"

"He's a creep."

"All he did was *dance* with her, Art. He doesn't even like her."

"It's not that," Art said firmly. "Tina and I have been shaky for a while. We would have broken up sooner or later. Saunders just speeded things up."

He was looking at his hands as he spoke, cleaning his fingernails, which were already clean. I didn't believe what he was saying about Tina. He was just trying to make the best of a bad situation. Then he looked at me.

"Will you do it?" he said.

"Do what?"

"Tell Saunders to go blow."

"I can't do that, Art."

"Why not?"

"I like him. He's a friend."

"Come on, pal. The only reason you hang around with him is to make him help you get a letter. I know how important it is to you. One of the other guys can help you do that. I can help you, too, now that I've got the time. Tell Saunders to go blow."

"You must be nuts," I told him. "You must have

lost too much blood and a bunch of your brain cells died."

I was furious. Art knew he'd gotten to me. He wouldn't keep from smiling. He was glad he had hurt me. I saw his bowie knife hanging in its case on the wall and knew where it really belonged. But I controlled myself.

"Well, you know where you can go, buddy," I said, and slammed the door behind me.

I made it home without anyone noticing me and locked my bedroom door. Thank God I had my own room and a good loud stereo system. After a while I felt better—good enough to think about what Art had said. And why he said it.

When I got into hockey, I made myself a promise that I would try to get a letter the first year. I didn't know if I could or not, but I figured it was possible. A letter's very important if you want to be anything in our school. Girls like guys who have letters. And college applications have a whole section where you're supposed to talk about the ones you've won.

But besides that, a letter's a sign that other people think you're doing a good job. And that, compared to other people, you can play the game pretty well.

Art was right—I did want help getting the letter. But he had never offered to help me. Buff gave me pointers without my even asking. So that made him a friend right from the start. We helped each other.

While I was thinking through all this, my father

was pounding on my door. The stereo was on so loud I didn't hear him until the record ended. I got up and apologized as I opened the door. Dad was already halfway back down the stairs.

"You've got a visitor," he said.

I went downstairs to see. It was Buff. He wanted to know how Art was. So I told him to come up to my room.

"He's really pissed off at you," I said. "And now he's angry with me, too. He won't be able to play for the rest of the season."

"I don't blame him for being mad," he said. "Too bad *I* didn't step on the bottle. Then we'd both be happy."

"I think you should stop bitching about playing hockey," I told him. I was angry with him for the position he put me in, even if it wasn't his fault. I found myself lecturing him the way my father lectured me.

"Either play or don't play," I said. "But stop talking about it. And stop blaming your father for what you're doing."

I got myself pretty steamed up. Buff shot up from his chair.

"OK, OK. Relax. Don't get yourself so worked up. And don't yell at me."

"Well, it's hard not being angry when your best friend blames you for something you didn't do."

"What do you mean?"

"Art thinks I helped you snake Tina away from him last night. He hates me. He doesn't want to be friends any more."

"Some friend."

"Yeah. He can be a real pain in the butt sometimes."

"And a real snob. He doesn't like you and me hanging around together, does he?"

I shook my head.

"I thought so," Buff said. And looked at the wall for a moment.

"It's pretty hard not to if we're both on the same line," I said. "Besides, I don't like him telling me who I can be friendly with and who I can't."

When Buff smiled at me I had to smile too. He leaned back in his chair with his hands behind his head and looked at me.

"Boy, I was feeling no pain last night," he said.

"I've got a good hangover myself," I said. "I can imagine how you must feel."

"I'm fine. I had a beer this morning. First thing. It makes a headache go away like that." He snapped his fingers.

"The last thing I want now is a beer," I said, and groaned when I thought about trying to skate. "I'm going to be dragging my butt at practice."

"You skate really fast," he said. "You're one of the fastest guys on the team, I'd say."

It was a nice thing for him to say. But we both knew I couldn't hang onto the puck for beans. I wasn't a very good shooter, either.

"Too bad they don't give letters for speed skating," I said, joking.

Buff sat forward and slapped me on the knee.

"Don't sweat it. You'll get your letter. All you need is confidence. And concentration."

"I could use a little talent too." I said.

"Talent's a God-given gift, my dad says."

"Maybe. But when you don't have much, practice is the next best thing. I think I need more ice time for practice."

"No, you don't. You've got a mental block. I had the same problem. You aren't used to handling the puck. You need more practice with your stick-handling."

I started thinking about it and realized that Buff, who'd already scored eight goals, spent most of his time shooting and passing during practice. Against Coach Anderson's orders, which is probably why he was demoted to third string.

"We could set it up out behind your garage," Buff was saying. "You could spend an hour or so a day shooting at targets."

"Set *what* up?"

"A shooting platform. I'll show you some shots. With a little practice you'll score your first goal in no time."

"Wouldn't it be nice?" I said. I could already see it, a slowly rising shot to the lower left-hand corner.

We got some paper and Buff drew some sketches of what the shooting platform should look like so we could get an idea of the kind of wood we'd need. Before he left that afternoon, Buff set a date to help me build it—the following Tuesday after school.

I was glad for the help. But I almost wished he hadn't offered to help me. Maybe I did like him just because of the hockey—the way Art said I did. I didn't think so. I liked Buff more than that. I figured we'd be friends a long time after hockey was over and even if I never scored a goal. But, as Coach Anderson says, you never know the final score until the game is over.

SEVEN

After Buff and I built the shooting target, he showed me how to make wrist shots and got me started with some shooting drills. I really got into it. Mom had to turn off the floodlights to get me to come in for dinner. She says I'm compulsive. Maybe so. The following day I came home to practice for an hour before I went to practice at Crystal. I lost track of the time and got there late.

Coach Anderson saw me come in. When he gets excited, his big fuzzy black eyebrows flap up and down.

"Good afternoon," he said. "The rest of the team is already on the ice." Flap, flap, flap. "Would you like to try some, too? Or are you maybe more interested in something else? Cars or girls or studies, perhaps?"

"I'm sorry I'm late, Coach."

"Yes. Well, for the next two hours I can offer you the exhilarating feel of high speed on two thin steel blades, the satisfying sound of hard rubber smacking against hickory, and the sensation of complete exhaustion which we call the game of hockey. I see you've heard of it? Good."

Coach could be very sarcastic sometimes. But I didn't mind. It was better than being yelled at. I got enough of that at home. As I laced up my skates, I told him about Art.

"I know. Why'd he go and do a cockamamie thing like that?"

I said I didn't know.

"It's too bad," he said. "Art's a good man. Hard to replace. So what I've done is to make d'Angelo a defenseman to take his place."

Andy d'Angelo was a second-string wing. He hadn't been playing well for several games.

"So who takes his place at wing, Coach?"

"Saunders. At least for the moment. I don't think he's got the right attitude, and his father drives me bananas. But he can score goals."

"Mr. Saunders was a star player in Canada, Coach."

"Don't I know it. And he's bound and determined to make his son one, too."

He looked at me and realized he was talking too much. I snapped the strap of my helmet and bent over to pick up my stick. Coach kicked me in the rear. "Now get out there and move those phalanges," he said.

I got on the ice in time for wind sprints. Sprints are about the only drill I do well at. So I enjoyed myself for five minutes. Then we started stickhandling exercises and I had to concentrate to keep from making a fool of myself. I barely succeeded.

Toward the end of practice, Tina and Julie sat down in the bleachers. Whenever Buff touched the puck or did a fancy maneuver, Tina yelled and clapped. Buff pretended not to notice. But when he skated to the bench, the guys whacked his pads with their sticks and laughed. That made him smile.

Coach blew his whistle for the final exercise, twenty times around the rink. Every time I passed Tina and Julie, I tried to imagine Buff in bed with Tina. Twenty times. Once Julie smiled at me and waved.

After laps I got off the ice and looked for Buff in the dressing room. He was sitting with a group of first and second stringers, most of whom were juniors and seniors. They didn't seem to mind he was only a freshman. They were discussing his promotion.

"Welcome back," Billy Martin said.

"It should have happened a long time ago," someone else said.

"Better late than never," John Murphy said. John is the captain of our team and a great defenseman. When he started to get undressed, everyone else did, too. My clothes were at the other end of the dressing room, but I didn't want to miss anything. I pulled off my jersey and sat down. Nobody seemed to mind.

It was the first time I'd been this close to John

Murphy and the rest of his friends. They all had girl friends and deep voices. I had never noticed what good swearers they were. I kept wondering if I would be able to act the same way they did by the time I was a senior. It didn't seem like I'd have enough time to become so self-confident. And so experienced.

"Hey, Sweeney," John Murphy said, scratching his crotch. "You get anything last night?" Sweeney was the first-string center. He had a bad case of acne, but he sure could score goals.

"I got *everything*, man," Sweeney said. Everyone around me chuckled knowingly. I knew what *everything* meant, but I didn't understand why it was so funny. But I laughed anyway.

"Who'd you go out with?" someone asked him.

"Carol Langulis."

The whole room erupted in laughter. Even I knew about Carol Langulis. She had had an abortion when she was fourteen.

"Crazy Carol," someone said.

"Double-jointed Carol," John Murphy said and nodded at Sweeney. "No wonder you were stiff."

"Judging from what I saw on the ice," Buff said, "he still is." Everybody laughed. John Murphy snapped the waistband of Sweeney's jockstrap.

"Look out, Sweeney," he said. "Saunders is already bucking for your position." Sweeney stood up and pointed at Buff, who stopped untaping his shin pads to listen.

"You've been cruising back there on the third line, Saunders," he said. "Eight goals come easy that way. But the last part of the season is the toughest part."

"Bethel, Old Town, and St. Luke's," Billy Martin said. "Even Milford will be tough."

"The pressure is on," Sweeney said. "You've got to play team hockey."

"And you've got to hustle the way Andy d'Angelo did," John Murphy said.

Buff nodded silently. When he looked up at John Murphy, he had a smile on his face.

"And while I'm doing that, do you mind if I do a little scoring?"

John Murphy laughed and punched his shoulder. "No shit, Saunders, you're a cocky bugger." Then he put on his parka, picked up his duffel bag in one hand and his three sticks in the other, and headed for the door.

"Where're you going, John?" Billy Martin said.

"Home for dinner and then Kelly's," he said without turning around. Kelly's was a favorite hangout for seniors and juniors.

"We'll meet you there at seven-thirty," Sweeney said.

John Murphy disappeared through the doors with a wave of his hand. Most of the other guys left soon after. After a while Buff and I were alone in the dressing room.

"For a guy with no confidence you're doing OK," I said. "You ready to go home?"

"Sure," he said. "I'll walk you partway."

We met Tina and Julie outside. It was snowing again. The ice in the parking lot looked like pools of black water. Tina gave Buff a big kiss and took his hockey sticks to carry. Julie fell into step with me. I carried my own sticks.

"You're a good skater," she said.

"Thanks," I said. "Next time you go running, let me know and I can watch and return the compliment."

"How about seven tomorrow morning?"

"I'm sorry, I have a date."

"You do? With whom?"

"My pillow."

She laughed and I looked ahead. Tina and Buff were walking faster than we were. When they saw how far behind we were, they stopped and waited. Tina threw her arms around Buff and kissed him. I don't think she missed Art very much. And I don't think she really liked Buff either. She was showing off, acting cool. Then Buff pulled a tiny bottle out of his parka pocket and gave it to Tina. She unscrewed the cap and drank it as we got closer.

"It's very sweet," she said.

"It's blackberry brandy," Buff said. "Try some."

"No thanks," I said. Julie nodded and Tina gave the bottle back to Buff. He drank what was left and threw the bottle into a snowbank.

"No, save the bottle," Tina said. "It's so small, it's cute." She started digging in the snowbank with her foot, looking for the bottle.

"Don't bother," Buff said. "I've got plenty more. Take your pick." He peered into the pocket of his parka. There were several miniature bottles of liquor—Old Crow Bourbon, crème de menthe, Dry Sack. You name it, he had it. "They're samples. My dad gets them from liquor salesmen. You can also get them on planes." He held one up in his fingers and winked at me. "Perfect size for a lunchtime pick-me-up."

"They *are* cute," Tina said. Buff gave her a couple, which she put in her purse. Then he gave her a few more.

"These are for emergency use only," he said. "In case I start feeling sick at practice or something. I'll tell you when I need them."

"Why would you feel sick at practice?" Julie said.

"Nerves. Ever since my accident I get a little tense and my stomach gets upset."

"At practice?" I said. "What's to get tensed up about at practice?"

"It helps me relax," Buff said. "I can concentrate better."

"The way you play now, you don't need to concentrate any harder," I said.

"You'll see," Buff said to me. "It helps you play better. Gives you self-confidence. You ought to try one sometime."

"Maybe I will."

Tina tugged on Buff's arm. "Come on," she said.

"I'm going to freeze to death if we keep standing around here. I've got to go home."

"OK," Buff said. He kissed her and waved good-bye to me and Julie. Then he headed for home in the opposite direction.

We dropped Tina off at her street and I walked Julie as far as her bus stop. While we waited for a bus to arrive, we joked around and threw snow at each other.

"Hey," I said finally.

"Hey, yourself." She took my arm.

"I've been meaning to ask you something."

"Go ahead."

"I was wondering if you'd like to study together some night. You know, for exams?" She must have been cold, because she was holding my arm very tight, trying to get closer to me.

"I'd like that," she said. "My parents have choir practice on Wednesday night."

"It's a deal, then," I said. "Let's kiss on it."

She looked up at me and closed her eyes. Right there at the bus stop. I closed my eyes, pulled her to me, and went for her lips.

All of a sudden a horn blared right in my ear. It was the bus. Julie gasped in surprise and twisted her head to see. My kiss hit her on the cheek.

"I'm going to miss the bus," she said and ran up the steps. The doors closed and the bus roared off so fast I had no time to jump out of the way when the wheels plowed through a slush puddle. My hockey bag was soaked. I picked it up, shouldered my sticks, and watched the bus go. Julie waved from the rear window until we couldn't see each other any more.

As I headed for home, I decided that the next time I tried, I would kiss her with my eyes open. That way I'd get her on the lips.

EIGHT

The next day I looked for Julie as soon as I got to school. I wanted to know if her parents would be going to choir practice and what time they would be back. But before I found her, Buff found me. He asked me to his house for dinner to celebrate his promotion to second string.

"Dad said to invite a good friend," he said, "so naturally I thought of you. Dad's got the night off on Wednesday. He's going to cook one of his specials."

Naturally. I tried to think up an excuse. Wednesday night was choir night. But the expression on Buff's face stopped me. He didn't know anybody else to invite. So I told him I'd be there by six.

I got there late. I was nervous. The stairs to Buff's apartment still smelled and I could hear the old lady with the cough. Buff's father greeted me at the door, singing at the top of his lungs.

"O-so-la-me-oh," he sang. He was wearing an apron and conducted an imaginary orchestra with a wooden cooking spoon. "Come in, come in," he said. "Buff is in the kitchen."

He didn't seem to be drunk.

A small round table was set up in the living room next to the windows. There was a white tablecloth and fancy plates and glasses. The candlelight made the silverware look gold. "The table looks great," I told Buff.

"I didn't do it," Buff said. "Dad did." He nodded happily at his father.

"Aw, that's nothing," Mr. Saunders said in a funny accent. "Now, look here, keeds. Get outta my kitchen so I can prepare ze special sauce."

"The secret sauce," Buff told me. And turned to his father, who was stirring the pot and sipping a glass of wine. "How much longer till we eat, Dad?"

"Feef-teen mean-oots."

"Good. I'll put the wine on the table."

Buff picked up the bottle and carried it to the table in the living room. Mr. Saunders started to sing again as Buff filled the three glasses on the table.

"Do you always drink wine with dinner?" I said.

"No. But this is a special occasion."

Buff took a big swallow of wine from his glass and looked at me. I put my glass of wine in front of my plate without drinking. Buff drank the rest of his, refilled his glass, and put it next to his plate. Then he sat down on the couch next to me.

"My dad says you aren't a man until you can

hold your liquor," he said. "But once you can, you can drink whenever you want. I can hold mine pretty well."

"Pretty well," I said, thinking about Tina's party. "But it doesn't make you any more a man than not drinking. My dad doesn't drink. And unless you know how to handle it, it could make you an alcoholic."

"My dad's been drinking like a fish since he was twelve, and he's not an alcoholic. Can an alcoholic sing like that?"

I didn't know. The only alcoholic I ever saw was a bum with a bottle of wine in a paper bag in New York City. We were on a field trip. Fourth grade. When the bum unzipped his pants to pee on the sidewalk, Mrs. Pitts screamed and tried to cover our eyes. There were twenty-four of us.

"How'd you know he took his first drink when he was twelve?"

"He told me. He tells me lots of things. Like growing up in Canada and Junior Hockey. We sit down with The Book and I ask him questions. He tells me stories. He worked in the oil fields in Oklahoma."

I didn't know much about my father, except that he flew thirteen missions over Korea with a broken finger. And he got all A's in the sixth grade.

"What's The Book?" I said.

Buff jumped up and got it. It was a photo album. He brought it to the table and we turned the pages. The pictures and clippings were about

Mr. Saunders mostly. His baptism notice, feature stories about him in Junior Hockey, and him and Mrs. Saunders.

It was a nice thing to have, I thought. A history of all the things, good and bad, that happened to you during your life. The way the articles and photos were pasted in and labeled told me that somebody had spent a lot of time on it. Judging from the handwriting, probably a woman.

"What do you think?" Buff asked.

"It's nice," I said. "I wish my family had one."

"My mother started it," he said.

He flipped The Book to the page with a black-and-white photograph of a woman and a child waving from the window of a sports car.

"That's Mommy when I was six."

She had blond hair and her name was Mary, according to the writing next to the photograph. And Buff had been blond when he was little. The other thing I noticed about the photograph was the car. It was good-looking—a sports car with little round side windows.

"What kind of car is it?" I said.

"A Thunderbird—1960," Buff said, lowering his voice so his father wouldn't hear. "My dad bought it because Mommy liked it so much. He still hates himself for listening to her."

"Why?" I said, wondering why he was talking so low.

"She died in it," Buff said. "They were on their way home from a party when a truck crossed lanes. Dad swerved. If his reflexes had been just a little sharper, he thinks maybe he could have made it."

I looked at the car again. A 1960 Thunderbird. It had to be the same one Buff had mentioned to Danny, the one that was in the shop when Danny asked to see it. Maybe Buff really did have a T-bird.

For a moment he looked like he was going to say more. But when he heard his father coming, he changed his mind and flipped to a new page.

"This is my section," he said. "Dad and I tried to make it just like his."

I could see they had. But Buff's part didn't look nearly as nice. The photos were wrinkled. The edges of the newspaper clippings about Buff's injury were jagged. And the handwriting was sloppy.

"You'll have lots of good things to put in here," I said.

"I hope so," Buff said.

"He'll have so many stories about his superstardom," Mr. Saunders said, "we'll have to get another book."

He was carrying a bowl of spaghetti with him. He went back for the sauce. It was hot and spicy-smelling. My mouth started to water. Buff got up to get the bread, and Mr. Saunders smiled at me.

"He's going to be a star, you know."

I nodded but didn't say anything. Buff sat down and Mr. Saunders filled our plates. We all started talking at once. It smelled so good.

After we packed a plateful away, Mr. Saunders

asked who wanted seconds and filled our plates again. Then he cleared his throat.

"I'd like to say a few words," he said.

"Hear! Hear!" I said.

"Speech, speech," Buff said. He refilled his glass. Then his father's. I didn't want any more. Mr. Saunders smiled.

"This is a very special occasion," he said, looking at Buff. "This young man, this fine hockey player, has been promoted to the second string." Buff and I smiled at each other. "In doing so, he has taken the first crucial step along the road to hockey greatness. For the first time, his skill and ability have been noticed. It won't be the last time. Buff, as you travel the road that leads to the top, you will have to overcome great obstacles. People will oppose you, luck will run against you. But you can always count on me to help you meet the challenges and overcome the obstacles. Together, the two of us can do it."

It was a nice speech. We drank to Buff. When I wiped my lips, I noticed that Mr. Saunders and Buff were smiling at each other. Things seemed to be working out a lot different than they had the last time I was here.

"You are going to be a star," Mr. Saunders said. Buff nodded and patted his arm. Then Mr. Saunders looked at me. "We're both glad you could come," he told me.

"I'm glad you invited me," I said. And I meant it. It was a nice thing for a father to do for his son, I thought. A little party to share something they both were interested in. The way my parents felt about my playing hockey, I couldn't imagine my father doing this kind of thing for me.

"What do you think of my boy's hockey?" Mr. Saunders asked me.

"Next year he'll be the best player on the team," I said.

"What'd I tell you?" Mr. Saunders said to Buff. "If you won't believe it from your old man, believe it from an impartial observer."

"He's no impartial observer, he's my friend," Buff said. His eyes looked a little glassy—with happiness, I thought. I nodded back at him. Mr. Saunders smiled.

"The best friends are the ones who tell it to you straight," Mr. Saunders said. "You are a very good hockey player. If only I could make you see it."

"Don't try," Buff said. "Tell us about Canada."

"He doesn't want to hear an old man," Mr. Saunders said. I sat up in mock surprise.

"Who says I don't?" I said.

"Tell about splitting the puck in two, Dad."

"It was nothing," Mr. Saunders said. "It happened all the time."

"Whenever the temperature got down around ten below," Buff said.

"We were playing outside," Mr. Saunders said. "Under lights. I picked up a loose puck, got up a good head of steam, and got by both defensemen."

"He was great at head fakes," Buff smiled.

"It was just luck," Mr. Saunders said. "Anyway,

there I was, one on one against the goalie with all the time in the world to shoot and win the game. I wound up and unloaded a real bomb from fifteen feet out." He paused. Buff refilled his glass for him. Then he continued. "The goalie never even budged. There was a big clang when the puck hit the post behind him. When he turned around to sweep the puck out, it was in two pieces."

"It was so cold the puck shattered," Buff said.

"It must have been a hard shot," I said.

"Happened all the time," he said. "But you're right, I did have a pretty hard shot."

"Can you believe it?" Buff said. "I'd love to be able to do that." He waved his arms excitedly. "Zip past the defense, crank up to shoot, and . . . POW!"

Buff's arm hit the edge of the table when he took his imaginary shot. His wineglass fell over, spilled on the tablecloth, and smashed on the floor. There was an instant silence.

Mr. Saunders sat back in his chair. Angry.

"I'm sorry, Daddy," Buff said.

"Look at that tablecloth. You've ruined it."

The wine was spreading out in a big pear shape. Buff was scared.

"Maybe I shouldn't have let you have wine with dinner," Mr. Saunders said. "Maybe you're not ready."

"I got excited, Dad."

I grabbed the salt dish and started to sprinkle it on the stain.

"The tablecloth will be OK," I said. "Salt gets out the wine."

Mr. Saunders grabbed my wrist. Suddenly I knew why he split pucks in two. He was strong, and he was hurting me.

"Don't touch that tablecloth," he said.

He squeezed my wrist harder. I dropped the salt dish. Then he got up and took the dirty dishes off the cloth. Without saying a word, he gathered up the cloth and took it out to the kitchen.

"What'd I do?" I said.

"Nothing," Buff said. "He gets mad real easily. But he doesn't mean it."

Buff bent over to pick up the rest of the dishes. I thought maybe he was going to cry.

"You all right?" I said.

He nodded.

"You can go home if you want," he said.

"No. Let me help you with the dishes."

I took some into the kitchen. Mr. Saunders was sitting on a stool next to the sink. The tablecloth was in his lap. He was scrubbing the stain with a wet sponge.

"Where should I put these plates?" I asked him.

Mr. Saunders looked up and nodded to the countertop next to him. I put the plates down and watched him scrub.

"You're a good boy," he said in tired voice. "Buff tells me you're a center. Third string?"

"Right."

"I was a center," he said.

When Buff came in, Mr. Saunders stopped

scrubbing and stood up. The tablecloth fell in a heap on the floor next to his feet. Buff bent over to pick it up.

"I'll finish cleaning it, Dad."

"Leave it alone," he said. "You'll only make it worse. I just realized I have to go to the shop. To check things out."

"Don't go, Dad. I'm sorry. Don't be angry with me."

"I'm not. But I've got to check on the shop. I'll be back later."

Mr. Saunders walked out without saying good night.

"He'll be OK," Buff said, turning on the water to wash the dishes. "He'll come back. He always does. He won't let me down."

"Why'd he get so upset?"

"He's fussy. Very demanding. And the tablecloth was one of Mommy's favorites. He's probably gone off to think about her."

"And get drunk?"

"Maybe. He really liked her. Everything went wrong when she died. He got hurt in a game. Then he got cut from the team. Then we started to move."

We were standing together at the sink, elbows pumping up and down as we washed. The suds sloshed over the plates, floating the spaghetti sauce away. Just like in the commercials. I was thinking about Mr. Saunders. I didn't like the way he treated Buff. He shouldn't have made him feel guilty about spilling the wine.

"I don't think your father was being very fair," I said finally. "Why are you always defending him?"

"My father's really a good guy," Buff said. "Strong as an ox. There's a photo of him throwing me in the air when I was ten. I must have weighed seventy pounds. But he never dropped me. Never."

"He must be awfully hard to live with though."

"We're both high-spirited," Buff said, wiping his eyes with the back of his hand.

"But he hits you, Buff. It must hurt."

"Not always."

Buff pulled the plug and the dirty water ran out with a sucking noise. He wiped his eyes again and spit in the drain. I'd never seen him look so miserable. And I wanted to know why.

"Why does he do it?" I said. "And why do you let him?"

"That's the way he is. He's always been this way. He's my father."

I tried to remember the one time my father punched me. I was ten.

"Haven't you ever wanted to run away?" I said.

"I've thought of it," Buff said in a quiet voice. "Maybe someday I will. But not until I'm older. My dad needs me now. He told me. I'm all he's got. We've got to stick together."

Later that night, at home in bed, I remembered what Buff said about his father. He never did say he loved him, only that they had to stick together. I figured that with his mother dead, Buff had to love his father, in spite of everything. There was no one else to love.

I tried to imagine how I would feel if my mother or father died. But I couldn't. They wouldn't die for a long time, not until I was all grown up. Another thing I couldn't imagine was calling my mother Mommy, the way Buff did. He must have been pretty little when she got killed. Maybe soon after the photograph was taken.

The next time I was at Buff's house, I'd ask to look at The Book again. I wanted to find out more about Buff's mother and how Buff felt about her.

NINE

I glared at the goalie painted on the plywood nailed to the garage wall. He was a dead duck.

"Go for the four," I told myself. I put the puck on the end of my stick and aimed at the space between the goalie's legs. I fired and the puck hit the four dead center. The goalie shook violently.

"Now the six," I said.

I fired again and a chip of wood flew up from the target. The boom echoed across our backyard.

"Gimme a one!"

"Boom!" Three inches off target.

"Hit the five!"

"Boom!"

"Try again with the rebound, dummy!"

"Boom!"

"Don't give up. You've got him worried."

"Boom! Boom! Boom!"

But I kept missing. I was getting tired. When I missed the plywood altogether and put another black gash in the garage siding, I decided to stop.

"All right, all right," I said. "Take a five-minute break."

I dropped the stick and cleared the snow off the back steps so I could sit down. I'd been practicing every day for two weeks since Buff's party. And the garage wall looked it. The marks could be filled in with wood putty and painted when it got warm. But Dad was bugging me to fix the broken windows now.

"They say that people who talk to themselves are either crazy," someone said, "or they have money in the bank. Which one are you?"

I turned around. It was Julie. "How long have you been spying on me?" I said.

She pushed herself off the fender of the station wagon and came over.

"I got here just as you scored the goal that won the Stanley Cup," she said.

That was the one that Bobby Hull almost deflected. He checked me into the snowbanks next to the garbage pail for revenge, but I had the last laugh. For a moment I was embarrassed that Julie had seen me acting like a kid. But she dropped the subject and picked up my hockey stick to try a few shots. She wasn't bad. I tried to imagine playing hockey in a skirt.

"What brings you over here?" I said.

"I just got my tickets to the recital," she said. "It's in two weeks at the Forum."

"Who's playing?"

"You wouldn't know him. He plays the flute."

"You're right. I wouldn't."

"I had to order them two months ago. His name is Rampal and he only comes once every two years. Last time I took my father. But this time I'd like you to go."

"I'm honored. When is it?"

"After the St. Luke's game. Eight o'clock that night. The performance is over at ten-thirty."

After the excitement of the St. Luke's game that afternoon, I didn't know how I was going to like sitting still and listening to a flute for two and a half hours that night. But I'd never tried it before. Don't knock it until you try it, they say.

"Maybe we could get a hamburger or something afterwards," I said.

"I wasn't sure you'd want to go," she said. "But I'm glad you can."

We had a date. It was as simple as that.

I picked up the hockey stick and took a few slap shots.

"You're getting pretty good," she said.

I wound up for another one as she looked behind her.

"What's that?" she said. "There. In the trees."

She pointed across the snowy backyard. Three dogs were barking and running along next to someone shuffling through the snow. After a second look I realized it was Ruth.

She's a cross-country addict. She took it up two years ago and she's good at it. You can tell when you see her ski. Her arms and legs move very relaxed as though she isn't even trying. But the dogs have to run like mad to keep up with her.

Ruth glided to a stop in front of us and bent over to take off her skis. The dogs dropped down in the snowbanks next to the garage pails to cool off.

"I heard all the noise and realized it was coming from your place," she said.

"We rigged it up a couple of weeks ago," I said. I took a shot to show her.

"It looks easy but it's not," Julie told her.

I introduced them, and Ruth took off her hat and mittens.

"Buff helped me build it," I said. "It was his idea, actually."

"Is he still the best hockey player in Chicopee?"

"He just made second string. We had a party to celebrate. Mr. Saunders made spaghetti."

"How was it?"

"The sauce was just a little too thick."

Ruth rolled her eyes at Julie.

"We had a pretty good time," I said. "Mr. Saunders was happy Buff made second string. But he sure jumps on him for the littlest things."

"How does Buff handle it?" Ruth said.

"When Mr. Saunders beats on him, Buff threatens to quit."

"But he still plays, doesn't he?"

"With a little help," Julie said.

She looked at me. I felt like I would be finking on him if I said anything.

"I'll tell her," Julie said. "Buff carries little bottles of liquor around with him," she said to Ruth. "We've seen him drink them. He calls them pick-me-ups. And he got really drunk at a party we went to."

"Tina's party," I said. Ruth nodded. "But he wasn't the only one who got drunk. Later he only drank one tiny bottle. He was showing off for Julie and Tina."

"Did you get drunk at Tina's?" Ruth said.

"No," I said, avoiding Julie's eyes. "Well, not really."

"Is Buff skipping school? Or sleeping in class?"

"I haven't seen him," I said. "But Art says he's been thrown out of math class for sleeping. Why do you ask?"

"Just wondering," she said.

She put on her mittens and hat. The dogs wagged their tails. Then she stood up and started to put on her skis. The dogs hauled themselves up out of the snowbanks and tucked in their tongues, waiting for her to start off again.

"I think he's just showing off," I said.

Ruth adjusted the straps on her ski poles.

"What do you think, Mrs. Benedict?" Julie said.

"He could be showing off," she said. "But Mr. Saunders sounds like one of those fathers who pushes too hard. Himself and Buff. Drinking is one way of coping with the pressure and tension."

"So is running. And hockey playing. And cross-country skiing," Julie said.

"There are lots of ways to handle it." Ruth nodded. "And they're all good as long as you don't overdo it. But when it starts changing the way you normally act, then it's too much. You've got a problem."

"Buff's acting pretty normal to me," I said.

"Good," Ruth said. The dogs whined and she planted her poles. "I better get going. Nice to meet you, Julie."

She pushed off on her poles. The dogs loped after her and started to bark. We could hear them long after she was out of sight.

"She's nice," Julie said.

"She's had a hard life," I said.

"Well, she certainly sounds like she knows what she's talking about. I'm glad I asked her about Buff. I hope you're not angry."

"I'm not."

"Maybe she's right about the drinking," she said. "What do you think?"

I'd been pretty busy trying to score a goal and get my letter. So busy that I hadn't talked to Buff or messed around with him since the party. What was he doing with himself? I didn't want to spy on him or anything. But I figured a phone call wouldn't hurt.

"Maybe we ought to give him a call," I said. "Come on."

We went inside. There was no answer at his place. My mother was cooking dinner and asked Julie to stay, even though it was a school night. Julie said yes without checking with her parents. She told us she's responsible for her own schedule because her running takes so much time.

My father likes responsible people. And when she told him about the Rampal concert, his eyes lit up. We never even got to the baked apple. He dragged her out to the den to listen to a Rampal album he knew he had somewhere. I listened for a while, too. It's a bunch of flutes and pianos who talk back and forth to each other. They sound a little silly, but it gives you a nice feeling to hear them. Julie's eyes were shining when the record ended.

I took her home. We didn't talk much on the way. It was cold and I was trying to think of a way to kiss her good night. Julie was humming. When we got close enough to see the lights on her porch, she gave me a hug.

"Buff's lucky to have a friend like you," she said. "You're a good person."

Then she gave me a little kiss on the lips. Just like that. Her cheeks were hard with the cold. But her lips were warm.

"You're a good person, too," I said. And I kissed her back. With my eyes open. It was easy kissing her. No sweat.

"When I saw you, I liked you right away," she said.

"I was flat on my back. In extreme pain," I said.

She smiled. I decided to kiss her again. Longer. And I wanted to slide my hands inside her parka and around her waist. She pushed up against me, so I did. When I touched her skin, it was warm. My heart was beating hard and I couldn't catch my breath. I wanted to lie down with her. Right there in the snow. I pulled her face away from mine.

"I want to be alone with you," I said. "Do you, too?"

"Yes," she said. "Oh, yes."

I had a big smile on my face, pleased she felt the same way. Julie took me by the hand and hustled us out of the light.

"Where're we going?" I said. My eyes were adjusting to the darkness. We were crossing her backyard.

"The garage," she said.

She slid the door up noiselessly and waved me through.

"Come on," she said.

I followed her in and there was the car. Big wide seats.

"Help me," Julie said. She was having trouble with the door. It wouldn't open. I tried all the others but they were locked.

"Damn." She held me tight and suddenly released me. "I'm going to explode," she said. She ran out.

"Wait a second," I said. "Where're you going?"

I caught up with her on the front lawn. "Lower your voice," she said, "or they'll hear you. I'm going to get the keys."

"You can't just walk in there, take the keys, and walk out again. They won't let you."

"If they don't, I'll die."

The front door opened and Mr. Seidman peered out. He nodded at me approvingly. "Home early," he said. "Did you have a good time?"

Julie looked at me and gave up on her plan. We walked to the porch.

"We had a lovely time, Daddy," she said.

"That's good," he said. "We're still up watching TV if you'd like to come in for a while," he told me.

"No thanks, Mr. Seidman," I said. "We have a double practice session tomorrow. I should be getting home. Call you tomorrow, Julie."

"See you," she said.

"Good night," Mr. Seidman said. And closed the door.

When the porch light went out, I decided I should kill myself. Instead, I jogged the eight blocks home and put the Rampal record on. It sounds silly, but it gives you a nice feeling.

TEN

I got two assists in the St. Luke's game. That means I passed the puck to the guy who took the shot that scored. Twice. Coach Anderson says that in his book an assist is as good as a goal. So I felt proud. We won 5–4. Everyone was clowning around in the locker room after the game. Everyone but Buff.

Buff had a crummy game against St. Luke's. They double-teamed him all game because they had scouted us. And they really roughed him up. When he fought back, the referee gave him a major penalty: five minutes for misconduct. Coach was furious. While Buff was in the penalty box, they evened the score. We went on to win the game, but all Buff could think about was his penalty.

"Don't let it get to you," I said, putting my socks on. "They were double-teaming you."

"But everyone's watching me now," he said, "waiting for me to make a mistake."

"It's only a game, Buff."

"Not for my father it's not."

I put on my parka and picked up my bag. The place was emptying out fast. I had to get home and get ready for the Rampal recital. Buff was still in his underwear. "Get dressed and I'll walk you to Murray Hill Avenue," I said.

"You go on," he said.

He gave me a tired wave and I left. Four blocks away, I remembered I'd forgotten the roll of tape I needed to fix my practice stick. So I went back. Buff was still on the bench. In his underwear. He had his back to me and didn't realize I was there. He opened one of his liquor bottles and drank.

"Why're you doing that?" I said.

He jumped about three feet off the bench when he heard my voice.

"Don't sneak up on a guy like that!"

"I didn't. I came back to get this." I picked up the tape from the bench.

"Now that you've got it you can go," he said.

"First answer my question."

"When I get home, my Dad will want to talk about the game. It's easier to take this way."

"I thought you said he didn't get drunk all the time."

"He doesn't."

"He's been drunk whenever I've seen him."

Buff started to get dressed in a hurry. "You've seen him twice."

"Want me to come home with you and make it three times?"

"You don't understand. This is a bad time for him right now at work. He takes it out on me.

But he'll make up for it in a couple of months. He won't drink at all. He goes on and off."

He looked down at his hockey bag. It was lying between his feet. He carried that bag with him everywhere. Most guys left theirs in their lockers. I gave the bag a kick and the bottles inside clicked together. Buff picked up the bag.

"Do you go on and off, too?" I said.

"Leave me alone."

"I don't want to bug you. I want to understand. Why do you do it?"

I don't think he knew the answer. Neither did I.

"It helps me relax," he said. "I take a couple of swigs and the fear goes away. You know those eight goals? Every one of them I was feeling nice. Not bombed but nice. Every one. The one time I played sober, I got my teeth knocked out."

"It was a freak accident," I said. "Drinking doesn't help you score. You aren't relaxed now, either. Look at you."

"I'll have one more and I'll be fine."

"What does your father think about it? Does he know?"

"Sure. He doesn't care. Just as long as I score."

"You've got more talent than anyone else on the team, Buff. You don't need to drink to score. You're great."

"My dad says I'm too small."

"The hell with your dad. He's so bombed he can't see straight. He never even watches you play. But the guys who play with you think you're the next Bobby Orr."

"I don't want to be the next Bobby Orr. And don't say that about my dad."

He stared at the floor again. Then he looked up at me. I could tell he was really torn up inside. Somehow it got to me. I felt I wanted to do anything I could to help him.

"You're just saying that about my playing to make me feel good," he said.

"No, I'm not. Look, I've got an idea. There's a pond near my house. We play pickup on it on weekend nights. Don't go home yet. Come on over to my place and we'll fool around on the pond for an hour or two."

Pond hockey is a different game. You don't need pads, and you can't even see the puck in the dark. Everyone can play and have a good time. A lot of guys are always out there. It would help Buff to let off steam, get back to normal more or less. I couldn't just leave him here.

I'd have time for this before I had to get ready for the concert. I was feeling less and less like going. And I thought Julie would understand if I didn't make it. If she saw Buff now, she'd probably want me to stay with him.

I found myself saying, "You can spend the night at my house afterwards." Getting away from his father for a while would sure be good for him.

Buff thought about it for a minute. "OK," he said. "But I've got to go home for a change of clothes first."

I didn't want him to go home alone, but I had to fix it up with Julie and my parents, now that

I'd suggested he stay over at my house. I was beginning to have a lot of second thoughts about what I'd gotten myself into, but it was too late to back out now.

"You'll meet a lot of good guys on the pond," I said. "I'll see you at my place at seven-thirty."

"OK. Your place at seven-thirty."

He started buttoning up his shirt. I got up to leave and saw the little bottle next to his leg. I wanted to take it away from him, but there wasn't much left in it anyway.

When I sat down to talk to my mother and father, I didn't want to get into a big explanation. It was too complicated and I didn't have time. So I tried to keep it simple. I started talking and my father started frowning. He always frowns when he doesn't get the message. Especially when he's trying to play gin rummy at the same time.

"Isn't he the boy who helped you with the target?" he said.

I nodded.

"Seems like a nice enough kid."

"But he's lonely, Dad."

The doorbell rang and my mother got up to answer it. Dad lit his pipe.

"That's probably him now," I said. "I've invited him to play pond hockey tonight and he's going to sleep over afterwards."

My father's pipe belched a thick cloud of smoke. "Are you asking us or telling us?"

We were getting off the track—and I was losing time.

"I didn't think you'd mind."

"I do. I do indeed."

"It's no big thing, Dad. I just asked him to spend the night."

"You *told* us he was spending the night."

"Let's just forget about the whole thing, then," I said.

Out of the corner of my eye I could see my mother in the hallway. She was waving to me.

"Don't you walk away from me when I'm talking to you," Dad said.

"Mom wants me."

"Sit," he said. Like I was a dog or something. He puffed on his pipe, looking at me.

"Arf, arf," I said.

He didn't get it. He opened his mouth just as Mom entered the room.

"Excuse me," she said.

She sat down.

"Just a minute, Margaret."

"You've got to show a little more respect for me," he said to me. "And your mother. This house is not a hotel."

"I don't mind making up the bed for Buff," she said.

"That's not the point, Margaret," he told her. "The point is that you and this house are not to be taken for granted." He puffed on his pipe. Then he frowned. "I thought you already had plans for this evening," he said.

"I was going to the Rampal concert with Julie. I think she'll understand. I have to call her."

"You don't have to call," Mom said. "She's in the hall."

My face flushed beet red. I could feel it.

"She looks very attractive, all dressed up like that," Mom said.

"I'll go talk to her," I said. "I'll explain."

Dad's voice made me stop. "What's going on around here, Margaret?"

When Julie walked into the living room, Dad laid down his cards without looking at me. He took his pipe out of his mouth.

"Good evening, Julie," he said.

She looked beautiful. When I looked at her, she looked so beautiful I wanted to die.

"Talk," Dad said.

"I'm sorry," I told Julie.

She nodded and tried to smile.

"I caught Buff drinking after the game," I told her. "Those little bottles?"

Julie nodded again.

"He's been drinking all along," I said. "Says they're how he scored his goals. They keep him relaxed so he can concentrate. Only he's not relaxed at all. You should see him. He's afraid to go home without drinking first."

"Why?" my father said.

"Because his father's always drunk when Buff gets there. They get into arguments and have fights."

"What kind of fights?"

"Fistfights."

My father took his pipe out of his mouth. "Real fistfights? About what?"

"Buff wants to quit hockey, but his father won't let him. He wants Buff to be a hockey star like he was."

"You've seen these fights?" my father said.

I nodded.

"You should have told us, dear," my mother said.

"Mr. Saunders sounds like a very sick man," my father said. "He could use some psychiatric care."

"Mrs. Benedict says Buff drinks because of the pressure," Julie said to my mother and father. "What do you think?"

"I think it sounds like alcoholism is what I think," my mother said.

"Now, Margaret, don't go off half-crocked," my father said.

"This is no time for bad puns," my mother said. "Something ought to be done."

"That's what I thought," I said. Hoping we could get back on the right track.

Dad looked at his watch. Then at Julie.

"It's twenty to eight," he told her.

She looked at me. "I think you did the right thing with Buff. You should stay here. I'll go by myself. But I've got to go now or I'll be late."

She was unhappy and disappointed, I could tell. But she appreciated what I was trying to do. That's what I'd thought. I walked her to the door.

"Call me in the morning," she said. "I'll be thinking of you." She left and I started back to the living room. I could hear Mom talking in a low voice with Dad. Low but fast. She was arguing with him. I made some noise and entered the room. They stopped talking.

"Can Buff spend the night?" I said.

"Of course he can," Mom said, and glared at Dad when he took his pipe out of his mouth. He looked at her and put it back in again.

"What time do you expect him, dear?" Mom said.

"He should be here any minute."

When I called him at eight-fifteen there was no answer. I figured he was on the way. I tried again at eight-thirty. Still no answer. I went out onto the porch for a while to wait. And to get away from my parents. Maybe he was getting beer again. I didn't want him bringing it in the house. Especially after what had happened with Julie.

"Damn you, Buff," I said. I kicked the porch railing.

I really didn't mean it. Buff had no idea that I had given up my first date with Julie to help him. He didn't even know I liked her. There were a lot of things we didn't talk about. Still, the least he could do was to call to say he wasn't coming. It was cold on the porch.

When I went back inside, the kitchen clock said nine-twenty. Then Dad came in looking for me. He saw the clock and the look on my face and put his arm around my shoulder.

"Come watch television with us," he said.

"There's a Charlie Chaplin movie on. *The Gold Rush.*"

My dad and I love Charlie Chaplin. One thing we have in common is a good sense of humor. But mine wasn't in very good shape right now. Even Charlie Chaplin couldn't make me laugh.

ELEVEN

I didn't hear from Buff the following day, which was fine by me. Sunday is supposed to be a day of rest anyway, and I needed some. I also needed time to square things with Julie. I took a copy of a book I read and liked with me when I went over to see her Sunday afternoon.

It was a warm day for March. We shoveled the melting snow off the seats of the swings in her backyard and sat down. Sometimes it's easier to talk about things outside, where you don't feel so closed in. I had wrapped the book in birthday paper. She was surprised.

"You didn't have to do that," she said. "I'm not mad at you any more."

"I know," I said. "I wanted to."

She pulled off the paper and smiled when she saw the cover. The book is called *The Babe*. It's about Babe Didrikson Zaharias, the athlete. She won three Gold Medals in the Olympics.

"Babe was a natural athlete," I said as Julie looked through the pages. "But the reason she was so great was that she pushed herself so hard. When she took up golf, she used to practice until her hands bled."

"Don't tell me any more," Julie said. "I'll read it and then we can talk."

"It's a great book," I said, excited by the thought of it. And getting a little off the track.

Julie folded up the birthday paper and laid the book on it in the snow. Then she started to swing again, humming to herself.

"How was the Rampal concert?" I said.

"Nice. It would have been nicer if you were there too. What'd you and Buff do—watch TV?"

"He never showed up."

"You're kidding."

"I haven't seen him since yesterday afternoon. And I'm not going to call him to find out. He can call me. I'm through worrying about him and his father. You'd think he was my brother or something."

Julie had stopped swinging and was clearing snow with the tip of her boot as she stared at the ground. It was her way of listening carefully.

"Maybe Art was right," I said. "Buff has been nothing but trouble from the word go. Maybe I don't need all this aggravation."

"He's your friend," Julie said. "He needs your help."

"But I don't know how to help him, Julie! I'm not a doctor. That's what my dad says he needs."

"Well, you have to do something. You can't ignore him."

"Maybe I should talk to Ruth again. She knows a lot of stuff."

Julie was thinking again, clearing an even wider patch around her swing.

"No maybes about it," she said. "Ruth and your parents say Buff and his father are under a lot of pressure. Drinking doesn't help it. You've got to find out what does."

"Will you help me?" I said.

She looked up suddenly. "Sure, you know I will. Why'd you even bother to ask?"

"Just checking," I said.

I kissed her. Then she gave me a long kiss back. But we figured her mother was probably standing at the kitchen sink watching us, so we knocked it off.

"What're you going to do about Buff?" Julie said afterwards.

"First thing to do is to find out why he never showed," I said. "We'll go from there."

Walking home, I felt better knowing Julie would help me. I called Buff several times Sunday night but got no answer. That bothered me. On Monday I waited for him in the corridor. We usually talked between the second and third periods. I had French in 208 and he had math in 210. But he didn't show. The bell rang and the doors closed and he still didn't show. I waited five minutes more and then went into class.

When Mr. Larsen saw me, he rolled his eyes. He hates it when we arrive late and interrupt him.

"Asseyez-vous," he said. *"Lisez la première phrase sur page soixante-dix-neuf."*

I stopped thinking about Buff and looked up at Mr. Larsen. He was waiting for me to answer.

"I'm sorry," I said. "I didn't understand the question."

A couple of kids laughed.

"Let's try something a little simpler then, shall we?" he said. "Repeat after me. *Peut-être.*"

"Poo-tet."

A couple more kids laughed.

"Non, non, non, monsieur! Peut-être!"

"Per-tetter."

"Non! Ecoutez-moi! Peut-être."

"Mr. Larsen, you better try someone else today," I said.

He stomped toward the front of the class in search of someone with a better ear for language.

I looked out the window again at the melting snow. The track was shoveled off and a gym class was running around it. They were wearing shorts and shirts in the warming air. Watching them, I couldn't sit still. I wanted to be away from school, away from hockey, running somewhere with Julie.

It was a much better idea than thinking about Buff. I kept rolling thoughts about him over and over in my mind. I didn't know how to help him. I couldn't help him the way he helped me—by building a target and practicing. His problem was much more complicated. And frankly, I didn't want to help him any more.

All of a sudden French class was in chaos. The

door flew open. Julie darted in in her gym shorts. She was breathing hard. The sight of her completely surprised me and Mr. Larsen, who shouted at her to stop. In French. She ignored him and the rest of the kids, ran to my desk, and grabbed me by the hand.

"Come. I've found Buff. Out by the tennis courts."

We raced out of the room, down the corridor, and broke into a dead run when we hit the fresh air. By the time we got to the tennis courts, four seventh-graders in gym shorts had found Buff, too. They were staring at him and laughing.

"He just peed in his pants," one of them said. And pointed at the dark patch spreading from his belt buckle to his knees. Buff was slumped on the bench, eyes closed.

"What's wrong with him?" one kid asked.

"He's sick," I said. I went to the bench to pull him up. Julie shooed the kids away.

"He's got mononucleosis," she said to them. "It makes you very tired. You guys get back to gym class now. We'll take care of him. Go on, get back on the track."

They left and I tried to get Buff to shape up. He groaned and his head rolled around like it was about to fall off. But I couldn't make him snap out of it.

"He is drunk, isn't he?" Julie asked.

"Yes. Very."

"Those kids are going to tell their gym teacher about this."

"I know," I said. "We've got to get him out of here."

I grabbed his arm, slung him over my shoulder, and tried to carry him on my back. He was heavy. Too heavy to carry very far. And his pee soaked my shoulder. I lowered him for a rest.

"We should get him to the hospital," Julie said.

"Let's get him off the field first," I said. "Then we can worry about that."

We each grabbed an arm and tried to drag him. His heels dug twin ruts in the muddy ground. We must have looked like three wounded soldiers. After a couple of yards, we had to drop him. He was too heavy.

"He doesn't look good," Julie said. "What're we going to do now?"

"We need a car," I said. "Somebody has to help us get him out of here."

Julie was getting nervous, panicky. Her eyebrows were knotted together, and she kept clenching her fists. I had to think of something fast or I'd get panicky too. Then I remembered Ruth. I fished in my pockets for a dime and gave it to Julie.

"I want you to call Ruth Benedict," I said. "Her number's in the book. Tell her we need help with Buff."

"OK." She dropped into her crouch to take off.

"I'll stay here with Buff," I said. "Hurry up."

She took off—legs flashing, arms pumping, a thin stripe of sweat down her back.

I sat down on the bench and looked at Buff. He

was huddled up in the mud on his side as though he'd been shot. Right in the middle of the day. All the anger I had been feeling drained out of me. How had I ever gotten involved with him in the first place? The only thing we had in common was hockey. Otherwise our lives were as different as night and day. Mine was easier, I figured. I could get out of my uniform aching and groaning to my parents, who helped make the pain go away in a couple of days. They supported me. So did friends like Julie, I guess. She helped, too.

But when Buff got off the ice, he was alone. Pain hurts more when you're alone. And Buff had to deal with a lot more of it than I did. Which hurts the most, I asked myself, losing four teeth or losing your mother? Getting smashed into the boards by someone who outweighs you by forty pounds or getting punched out by your father? Maybe if you're all alone, the way Buff is, there's no difference at all. Everything hurts the same and shows in your eyes. Or maybe it's like what the intern told us in the hospital when he was stitching Buff up—when you get hurt real bad, all the nerve endings get knocked out for a while and you can't feel a thing.

I remember when the doctor came out of my grandfather's hospital room when I was nine. He had his head down and was wiping his glasses. When he looked up, he couldn't face my father, so he looked at me.

"Your grandfather's dead, son," he said. "The heart attack came on so fast he never felt a thing."

Buff couldn't feel a thing, either. I sat down next to him in the mud and patted his head. I had to concentrate to keep myself from crying. By the time Julie got back, I was OK. But I felt tired and sad. I knew he wasn't dead. But part of him was dying.

"She says she'll be here as fast as she can," Julie said. She was breathing hard. She looked at Buff again.

"Has he been like that the whole time?" she said.

I nodded.

"Boy, he must be really loaded."

Then Buff groaned. We jumped about ten feet in the air and backed away from him. Buff swore out loud, and his left leg kicked out twice.

"Oh, my Lord," Julie said. "He's going to die."

But I didn't think so. I was more worried about him swallowing his bridge than dying.

About fifteen minutes later Ruth honked her horn once as she entered the parking lot. Julie ran over to her and told her to drive onto the field. By the time Ruth got there, Buff was quiet again. She stood over him and stared at him for a moment. Then she bent over.

"Come on, Buff," she said. "Up and at 'em."

Buff smiled with his eyes closed, as though he was having a good dream. Ruth lifted his eyelids.

"We found him like that," I said. "Twenty minutes ago."

"I think he's OK," she said. "Just very hung over and completely exhausted. He was probably unconscious for a while." She inspected his face and mouth.

"Come help me," she said. I bent down next to her. "We're going to pick him up and get him walking," she said. "But first I want you to hold him up like this."

Ruth hoisted Buff into a sitting position. I put my arm around Buff's shoulder to keep him from falling over while Ruth checked his arms, then his scalp.

"What are you looking for?" Julie said.

"I want to be sure he doesn't have any serious injuries before we move him," she said. "He's got a big bruise on his cheek. God only knows where he got it."

Ruth checked him out all over with smooth, careful hands. When she discovered he had wet his pants, she said nothing about it. Then she was done.

"He looks okay to me," she said. "Let's see if he can walk to the car." The three of us dragged Buff to his feet and guided him to the station wagon.

"Don't look so sad," she told me. "I'll take him over to my house and get him cleaned up."

We worked him into the cargo area of the station wagon and slammed the door. I looked at Ruth.

"If he goes back to his father, it's going to happen again," I said. "We've got to keep Buff away from him."

"Well, you can't take a son away from his father," Ruth said. "Not very easily anyway."

"Maybe you could talk to Mr. Saunders?" Julie said. "You know what you're doing."

"I can't do that. He's not going to give me the time of day."

Buff was moving around in the station wagon now, moaning and groaning. We stood there and stared at each other. When the bell rang, Julie stirred.

"Fourth period," she said. "Here come the kids."

She looked at me. "Look," she said. "I think Mrs. Benedict's right. We can't tell Mr. Saunders what to do. Buff is his kid."

"But don't you see?" I said. "He's ruining Buff."

"The person who should talk to Mr. Saunders is Buff," Ruth said. "And he's in no shape to do that right now." She got into the car and started it up. "Let me take him home. You come over after school and we'll talk to him then."

A couple of kids walked by and peered in the windows at Buff. He was curled up in a ball.

"You'd better let Ruth go," Julie said, "or it'll be all over school in ten minutes." She nodded over her shoulder at the three girls approaching us. Brownie Thompson, Bev Kimberly, and Sugar Wright. The Three Mouthkateers.

Ruth shifted into gear and pulled away. Julie and I waved nonchalantly and then walked toward them.

"What're you doing in your gym clothes, Julie?" Brownie said. "That the only way you can catch him?"

The other two laughed. Julie just ignored them.

When I got to history class, I was late again. Mrs. Watts asked me why. I said I was unavoidably detained but hoped I wasn't too late. I was told to sit down and turn to page forty. I did.

But I couldn't concentrate the rest of the day. The sight of Buff peeing in his pants kept bugging me. Getting that drunk was like killing yourself. Why would anybody want to die at fifteen?

My parents kept telling me that life was just starting to take off. Pretty soon I'd get my driver's license, go to college or get a job, fall in love. There was so much to look forward to.

But Buff couldn't be getting that same message from his father. He was getting a different story. And it didn't have a happy ending. All of a sudden it hit me. Mr. Saunders was the problem. Not Buff. If we could keep Saunders away from Buff, we'd have a chance to help Buff.

Right after class, I decided, we'd pay a little visit to Mr. Saunders. Me and Julie.

TWELVE

"Mr. Saunders is in his office," the bartender told us. He pointed to the door next to the jukebox at the far end of the dance floor. "Through there and down the corridor to the end," he said. He looked at Julie and me. "But you can't go in there now. He's got a salesman with him."

I was about to argue with him, but Julie cut me off.

"We'll wait here for him if you don't mind," Julie smiled.

"Sure thing." The bartender went back to cleaning glasses.

We were both nervous. I didn't think Ruth would approve of what we were doing. I had had to do some fast talking to get Julie to come with me. But we were here. Mr. Saunders would have to hear us out. I figured he could talk to a salesman anytime, so when the bartender went in back, we slipped through the door and down the corridor. The sign on the door said "Edwin Saunders—Manager." We pushed inside.

Mr. Saunders was in his shirt sleeves. His feet

were propped up on the desk. Across the desk from him was the salesman. He had a suitcase full of bottles next to him. He was refilling Mr. Saunders' glass. When he saw the expression on Mr. Saunders' face, he twisted around in his chair to look at Julie and me.

"We've got to talk to you, Mr. Saunders," I said. "It's about Buff."

Mr. Saunders blinked at me. Maybe he didn't remember who I was. Maybe he was too surprised to say anything.

"What do you say, Ed?" the salesman said, ignoring us, trying to finish his pitch. "Six ninety-five a bottle, eighty-nine dollars the case."

Mr. Saunders shifted his stare from me to the salesman.

"Leave us alone, George, would you?" he said.

"What about the order?"

"Forget the order. Leave us alone."

George was angry. He closed his sample case and left in a huff. When he slammed the door, Mr. Saunders motioned us to sit down.

"Where is he?" Mr. Saunders said.

"Julie found him on the field at school today," I said.

"He was unconscious," she said.

Mr. Saunders didn't say a word.

"He was supposed to spend the night at my house on Saturday," I said. "He was worried about getting into a fight with you about the game."

"I thought he was with you," he said.

I knew he was lying. He wouldn't look me in

the eye. He'd done something to Buff—beat him up probably.

"Come on, Mr. Saunders," I said. "We're not stupid."

Mr. Saunders decided he didn't like me.

"Where is he now, son?" He was getting angry. Any second he would start yelling at me.

"Please listen to what he has to say, Mr. Saunders," Julie said. "Just for a minute. Buff is our friend."

"I'm going to count to three and you're going to tell me where he is," Mr. Saunders said. He got up, his hands gripping the edge of the table. Julie started backing toward the door.

"One!" he said.

"Come on," she said. "Let's go."

"Two!"

Mr. Saunders saw my eyes dart toward the door when Julie opened it. He grabbed me by the neck. Julie screamed. He clapped his hands on either side of my face and lifted me off the ground. My spinal cord popped. He pinned me against the wall.

"Tell me where he is!" Saunders shouted. Whiskey breath in my face. "Talk!"

I couldn't. His grip was grinding my jaws together. My face was so squooshed I could hardly breathe. Mr. Saunders tried to smile. And he tightened his grip.

"You're a nice boy," he told me. "I know you want to help him. So tell me where he is."

I wouldn't. He pulled me away from the wall. Closer to his face.

"Please?" he said.

I wouldn't. So he jammed my head against the wall. Julie yelled and picked up a chair. It hurt but I didn't cry out. It's impossible to cry in that position. Mr. Saunders pulled me away from the wall again.

"Tell me," he said, jamming my head against the wall again.

It didn't hurt the second time. But there was a loud ringing in my ears and a flash of red light so bright I had to close my eyes.

"Ruth Benedict's house!" Julie screamed. "Seventeen Woodland Road! Now let go of him!"

When she swung the chair at him, Mr. Saunders let me go. I slid down the wall to the floor. Saunders grabbed the chair out of her hands and threw it at the wall next to her. It shattered like glass three inches from her face. Then he pushed her aside and headed for the door.

"You bully!" Julie screamed. "You drunken bully! Look at him! Look what you've done!"

She pointed at me. I was having a little trouble trying to stand. My legs kept arguing with me about which way we were supposed to go. And my head was making strange squeaky noises. So I sat down again and felt for the lump on my scalp.

Mr. Saunders stopped at the door and looked back at me. "Nobody comes between me and my boy," he said. "Nobody."

Then he left, slamming the door behind him. I would have preferred it if he'd done it a little more quietly. My ears were still ringing. But nothing seemed to be broken. It's a good thing I have a hard head. Julie helped me to a chair. I sat down to catch my breath.

"Are you all right?" Julie kept asking me. "Are you OK?"

"If I'd been a little faster on my feet, I could have kicked him in the balls," I said. "That would have stopped him."

I always think of better ideas afterwards. When I'm recovering.

"Do you want me to call an ambulance?" Julie said.

I must have looked pretty bad to her. But we didn't have time for that.

"No," I said, "call a cab. We've got to get over to Ruth's."

THIRTEEN

Ruth and Buff were in the small bedroom playing gin rummy when we got there. Ruth's house is small to begin with, the right size for one person. But with the four of us in the bedroom together, it was crowded. The bed took up most of the space.

Buff was in bed, wearing an old bathrobe—Ruth's, I guess. She had cleaned him up, washed and dried his clothes, too. But he still looked terrible. His skin was pasty white, and he had big circles under his eyes. The bruise on the left side of his face was light purple. Ruth had propped three pillows behind his back so he could play cards properly. She was really pampering him, I thought. For a moment I wished I was in bed, not him. But I was relieved to see that Mr. Saunders wasn't there. And that Buff was in a good mood. He smiled as he tried to decide which card to throw down. Ruth was ready to make her next play. She was so impatient she didn't even notice me.

"Sit down, sit down," she said. "I'm just taking this sucker for every cent he's got."

She snatched up Buff's discard and threw down one of her own. They were getting along together very well.

"How're you feeling?" I asked Buff.

"Until I started playing cards with this shark, I was fine," he said.

His voice was weak, but he laughed.

"Shark? Why, Buff, honey, I'm just a sweet little old lady living out my days on Social Security."

"And your gambling winnings."

Ruth cackled and pounced on another discard. She shuffled cards around and then threw down her hand.

"Gin," she said.

Buff grimaced as she picked up her pencil to count her points.

"Let's stop now," he said. "I can't take any more. How much do I owe you?"

Ruth finished counting, double-checked her math, and then looked at him with a smile.

"Fifteen hundred and three bucks," she said.

"Will you take a check?" he said.

We all laughed. Buff leaned back against the pillows as Ruth gathered up the cards. As she did, she got a better look at me.

"What hit you?" she said.

"We went to see Mr. Saunders," I said.

"Mr. Saunders beat him up," Julie said. "To find out where Buff is."

"You shouldn't have gone there in the first place," Buff said angrily. "You should have stayed out of it. It's my business."

When he said that, I flipped out. I started to yell at him.

"That's where you're wrong, buster! It's everybody's business! Mine! Ruth's! My parents'! Julie's! Everybody's! Do you realize how many people are involved in your problems? Do you?"

Buff stared at me without saying a word.

"I want an answer," I said.

Ruth cleared her throat. "Buff and I have been talking about that all afternoon. A lot happened to him this weekend. You two guys could do with some talking between yourselves."

She nodded to Julie, who stood up. Buff stared at the sheets until they were out of the room. When the door closed, he looked at me. I didn't speak until I was sure I could do it without yelling.

"Tell me what happened," I said finally.

"We got into another argument," he said in a low, tired voice. "So I said I was going to leave him. He gave me ten bucks to do it and he walked out on me. He said he didn't want a quitter around."

"Where were you going to go?"

"Toronto. My aunt lives up there. I went to the bus station, but they didn't have another run until Monday, early. So I went back home."

"Why didn't you come over to my house then? Like we planned?"

"It was late. And I wanted to talk to him again."

I didn't say anything about the concert and Julie. It didn't matter any more.

"What happened next?"

"On Sunday I asked him for more money. But he wouldn't give it to me. We got into a big fight."

Buff pointed to the bruise on his face.

"I hid in a garage I know for most of the day. When he went to work, I snuck in for some food and clothes. Money, too. Then I went back to the bus station."

He stopped talking when the door opened and Ruth walked in. I could hear Julie on the phone in the living room talking with her parents. Buff wiped his eyes as Ruth sat down on the edge of the bed to listen. She smoothed a loose strand of hair on his forehead and patted his cheek. She'd already heard the story once.

"I don't know how I got to school the next day," he said. "All I remember is I hid out in the men's room at the Gulf station next to the bus terminal. It was warm in there. I drank a bottle of wine and thought about things. And I decided not to wait for the bus. I started walking."

"To Canada?"

"It seemed like a good idea at the time. It still is. I'm not going back to him."

He swung his legs over the bed, put on his shoes, and threw off his robe. So I grabbed him by the arm.

"You can't leave now," I said. "You're sick."

Buff looked at me and slowly removed my hand from his arm.

"I'm not leaving tonight," he said. "I'm going to the bathroom. I've got to take a whiz."

"Sorry," I said.

When Buff left the room, I turned to Ruth. "Do you think he means it?" I said.

"They've been at each other for a long time," Ruth said. "But if Buff had really wanted to leave, he wouldn't have gone back to his father to ask for more money. He would have stolen it or borrowed it from you."

"And I would have given it to him, too," I said. "Anything to make him change. He could kill himself drinking like that, couldn't he?"

"He could," Ruth said. "Eventually."

Then I realized that Julie was standing behind me in the doorway, listening to Ruth and me talk.

"You knew Buff was a drinker the whole time, didn't you?" she said.

Ruth nodded. Then it dawned on me.

"Did you ever have a drinking problem?" I said.

"Used to. Not now. Not for ten years."

"Did it happen when you were married to Tommy?" I said. She nodded again. "Why is it so hard to stop?"

"When you use booze to get yourself through a bad time, you never quite make it," she said. "It takes too much out of you. So you make promises to yourself. Promises about how you're going to take just one more eensy-teensy drink. But they're promises that nobody else knows about. Or cares about, maybe. It's too easy to break that kind of promise."

We all heard a noise and turned to listen. I thought it was the sound of the plumbing in the bathroom. It came from that direction. After a moment of silence, though, I figured I was hearing things.

"So what do we do now?" I said.

"Tonight, nothing," Ruth said. "I told Buff he can stay here if he doesn't want to go home. Tomorrow I'm going to take him over to the hospital to check out the rehabilitation program. He wants to quit. But he can't shake the monkey off his back without help. No one can do it alone. He and his father both ought to enroll in the program."

"But Mr. Saunders has been drinking for a long time," I said. "He's not about to quit, from what I can see."

"Well, I'll talk to him. He doesn't realize that Buff is at the end of his rope," Ruth said. "Buff's going to get help. And he's not going home until his father does too."

Then we all heard it—somebody yelling outside. I jumped up from the bed when I heard Buff yell back in the bathroom. We were there in a flash. The bathroom window was wide open. I could see Mr. Saunders in the snow outside the window. In his shirt sleeves. He must have stopped at a bar before coming to Ruth's.

"Come on out, Son!" Mr. Saunders yelled.

"Shove it!" Buff yelled back.

He slammed the window when his father started

to laugh. Then Buff raced past me, into the living room, and locked the front door. Then to the kitchen for the back door.

"You don't have to do that," Ruth said. "I won't let him come in if you don't want him to."

"He's crazy now," Buff said. He listened as his father yelled again, this time in the front yard. "He could hurt you. He isn't thinking straight."

When Mr. Saunders yelled again, we went to the bay windows and opened the curtains. He was standing in front of the hedges under the window, holding a barbecue grill from the backyard in his arms. When he saw us, he raised the grill over his head.

"Either he comes out or I come in!" he yelled. "Which will it be?"

Ruth pulled us away from the window.

"Do you think he'd really do it?" Julie said. "Break in like that?"

"My father could do anything when he gets like this," Buff said.

He picked up the telephone and started to dial. "He's crazy right now, I'm telling you," he said.

"Here Buffy-Buffy-Buffy!" Mr. Saunders yelled. He tried to whistle through his teeth but was too drunk to make the right sound. So he started to laugh. "Come on out, Buffy-Buff!"

Ruth pulled us away from the windows again. "I want you all to stay back," she said. "He doesn't need any encouragement. Buff, what are you doing?"

"Calling the police," he said.

"Put that phone down," Ruth said. "You're not helping one bit."

"Yes, I am!" he said. "I'm helping me. I should have done this a long time ago!"

The police station answered.

"Hello?" Buff said. "Yes, I want to report a drunk outside my window. I want you to get rid of him."

"Buff, put down the phone," Ruth said. "We can handle this."

Buff hesitated, taking the receiver away from his ear as Ruth approached him. She stuck out her hand for the phone.

"The police will only make things harder," she said softly.

But as Buff put the phone in her hand, Mr. Saunders threw the grill at the window. The panes shattered, the grill bounced off the cushions of the couch, and Ruth screamed. The grill rolled out onto the rug, spilling ashes everywhere. We were all stunned. Ruth stared at her rug. There was glass all over it. Mr. Saunders was doubled over in the yard, laughing so hard he was hugging himself.

"I told you, I told you," he kept saying.

Buff took the phone back from Ruth. He put it to his ear.

"Yes, I'm still here," he said calmly. "His name is Edwin Saunders. . . . Yes, I can identify him. He's my father."

Mr. Saunders staggered to the hedges and tried to climb through them and into the house. He kept yelling at Buff to get off the phone. So Buff turned his back on his father and put a finger in his free ear so he could hear the desk sergeant's questions.

"Seventeen Woodland Road," he said.

Mr. Saunders bent over and made a snowball. He aimed for Buff's back but hit the window frame, he was so drunk.

"Come on, Buffy-Buff!" he yelled.

He made another snowball and aimed again. This one hit Buff in the shoulder as he was hanging up. It wasn't a hard throw, but when Buff turned around, he was mad. As though something had snapped. He slammed the receiver down on the hook and was outside in the snow in an instant. Mr. Saunders saw him coming. He dropped the snowball he was making and turned as Buff charged him. Buff tackled him around the waist, burying his head in his father's stomach and knocking him flat on his back. They wrestled in the snow for a moment, but Buff got on top, pinned his father's shoulders down with his knees, and cocked his arm to punch him in the face. But then, for some reason, he hesitated.

"Go on!" Mr. Saunders said. "You got me!"

Buff's fist knotted tighter. But he paused again.

"Hit me!" Mr. Saunders said. "You hate me, don't you?"

Buff nodded. "Yes, I do."

"Well, get it out of your system," Mr. Saunders said. "For once and for all. Hit me."

Buff shook his head. Mr. Saunders worked one

hand free and grabbed Buff's wrist, slapping himself across the face with his son's hand.

"Is that how much you hate me?" he said. "Is that it?"

"I hate you more than you'll ever know," Buff said.

"Show me, Son. Show me how much."

Buff refused. He started to get off his father's chest. Mr. Saunders grinned.

"You're a sissy," he told Buff. "A mama's boy. I always knew you were a mama's boy."

Buff turned around, made a fist, and punched his father in the face. Mr. Saunders grunted, then laughed at him.

"Just like a mama's boy."

Buff hit him again. And Mr. Saunders laughed.

"Stop it!" Julie screamed.

Ruth grabbed her by the shoulders and whispered something in her ear to make her stop. I couldn't keep my eyes off Buff. He was beginning to cry. Using both hands to fight, he put his weight behind the punches and grunted with the force of the impact.

"Is that it? Is that it?" Mr. Saunders kept saying in a high, thin voice. "Is that it?"

There was a cut on his lip and his voice was trembling, but he never took his eyes off Buff. Buff hit him in the face and chest until Mr. Saunders touched his fingers to his lips and saw his own blood.

"Is that it?" he said in a weak voice. "Is that it?"

"No!" Buff said. "No, it's not."

He tried to catch his breath so he could keep punching. I could tell he wanted to keep hitting his father. There was more hate to get out. But he couldn't keep going. He was too tired. He looked up at me and groaned, as though he was trying to speak but couldn't find strong enough words. He was done.

Mr. Saunders pushed him off. Buff rolled over, then got up. Ruth rushed to him, throwing her arms around him protectively, trying to steer him toward the house. But he staggered away from her. He started to run toward the street. People were out of their houses by now, and the sirens were wailing on their way to Ruth's. I didn't know what to do.

"You better go after him!" Ruth said.

FOURTEEN

I trailed him for four blocks—across Murray Hill Avenue toward the bus station. He was walking fast, breaking into a run when he looked around and saw me. But I wasn't as tired as he was. He couldn't shake me. I figured I'd let him run himself down before I got closer. He was still pretty angry.

It's creepy around the railroad station at night. Bums live in the doorways of the buildings. Twice they shouted stuff at me—exactly what they said I'm not sure. They sounded like they had socks on their tongues. I put on a little speed to close the distance between me and Buff. It's a good thing I did, because I almost lost him in the shadows. I wasn't watching him too closely because I figured he was heading toward home. All of a sudden he wasn't there. He just disappeared.

I slowed down, then stopped dead and looked around. One side of the street was a block-long warehouse. The other side had a couple of burned-out houses and a bunch of alleys. The only place he could have gone was down one of those alleys.

They were dark, pitch-black. So before I started down the first one, I waited until my eyes adjusted to the light.

When I could see better, I realized I wasn't in an alley, really. It was a driveway to a garage set well back from the street. The garage door was windowless. But there were several sets of footprints leading to and from the door. No tire tracks, but plenty of footprints. So I knew Buff was in there.

I put my ear against the garage door. Not a sound. I knocked with one knuckle and waited for him to answer. There was no answer, but I knew he was in there. I could practically feel him breathing on the other side of the door. So I knocked again. Two knuckles this time.

"Go away!"

"Come on, Buff! Let me in! It's cold out here!"

"I said go away!"

"I will. But first let me make sure you're OK."

"I'm fine, I tell you. Now beat it."

"Not until you listen to me. I'm sorry about your father. I was trying to help."

"I know that."

"I figured he'd listen to me."

"My dad never listens to anyone. I realized that tonight. We could fight forever and he wouldn't hear what I'm saying. It's hopeless."

He started to cry, moan as though he was dying. I'll never forget the sound. I rapped on the door.

"Hey, Buff! Let me in!"

When the lock sprang open, I lifted the door

high enough to scramble under. Buff was still crying as he leaned on the door to close it. I could barely see him, it was so dark. It was just as well. Buff couldn't stop crying. I sat down next to him. I'm not much good at comforting people. I don't know what to do or say. But I had to do something or I was going to start crying too. So I put my hand on his shoulder and squeezed it.

"Go on," I said. "Cry as long as you want."

He threw his arms around me, knocking me backward into the door, and buried his head in my shoulder. For a minute I thought he was going to beat me up. I was so surprised I started to laugh. He was hugging me tight and crying.

"Don't worry, it'll be OK," I said finally. "Everything'll work out."

The door lock was digging into my back. And Buff is no lightweight. Finally he let me go, which made me a little more comfortable. I kept talking to him, saying the same thing over and over. It didn't matter so much what I said as how I said it. Eventually he stopped crying. I could see his breathing slow down, and then he seemed to relax. As though he was falling asleep. And after a while I think he did doze off.

It was warm in the garage—smelly with oil and leather and paint. I slid away from Buff and stretched, reaching out in the dark cautiously to find out where I was. I felt along the garage door to the corner and found a light switch. When I flicked it on, a bare bulb overhead made me blink for a second. Then I saw the car.

It was a 1960 T-bird. A white one with red interior. The one in the photograph in The Book. The grille was missing. And the left front fender had a large patch of gray primer on it. But the rest of it was flawless flowing curves of eggshell white. Someone had spent thousands of hours on this car. Everything smelled new, even the red leather seats. There was a package of road maps on the front seat. And a canvas bag in back. Buff's bag.

"Looking for these?" he said.

He had poked his head in the driver's window and was wiggling the car keys at me. I pulled my head out of the window on the passenger's side and stood up, looking at him over the roof.

"It's beautiful," I said.

Buff jumped into the driver's seat. He put the keys in the ignition and gave the rear-view mirror a minor adjustment. Then he leaned back in the driver's seat and closed his eyes. He had a big smile on his face. He seemed like a different person.

"It sure is," he said.

"Who fixed it up?"

"My dad. It was a complete wreck so he's had to completely rebuild it. It's taken him years. There's more money in this car than in Fort Knox. He works on it when he's on the wagon. Get in if you want."

I did. The seat was firm and comfortable. Buff turned on the radio and tapped out the beat of the music on the rim of the steering wheel.

"It must be almost finished," I said.

"It is. I was going to wait until he had it perfect, but now it doesn't make much difference. The engine runs like a clock. I'll fix the little stuff when I get to Toronto."

I believed him. He had the whole thing planned. It was the best way to get back at his father. I knew if I argued with him, it wouldn't do any good.

"He thinks he'll bring her back if he makes it perfect. The way it was before the accident," Buff said. And snorted sarcastically. "He really does. But nothing's gonna make up for what happened. Nothing. I've told him that a hundred times."

His eyes were watering. I knew he was thinking about his mother. Imagining all the great things mothers do for their kids. Not just hugging and kissing them, but talking and playing with them. Making them feel safe and happy. Loving them, I guess. I didn't blame Buff for hating his father, not after what he did to me. And not after seeing this car. Mr. Saunders put more love into one fender than he gave to Buff. You could see it in the shine. Everything in the car shone. Even the ashtrays. He must have really loved his wife. And he must have felt very guilty about the accident.

"Was your father drunk when it happened?" I asked.

"Three guesses," Buff said dryly. "If he hadn't been such a big-wheel hockey player, he would have been thrown in jail for what he did to her. The wrong person died."

Buff stared at the dashboard for a moment, flicking something away from the speedometer.

"It's about six hundred miles from here to Toronto," he said. "I figure it'll take me about twelve hours."

"That's a lot of driving," I said.

"I know. I'll stop for coffee every hundred miles or so. Get out and stretch my legs."

I nodded. He started to shift the gears, working the clutch and gas pedal expertly. I wondered how many hours he'd spent sitting in this car.

"The weather's still pretty cold," I said. "Roads will be bad. Maybe you should wait until spring."

"Can't wait. I don't have any place to stay any more."

"Ruth wouldn't mind for a little while. And my parents will help. I'll talk to them."

"There'd only be more trouble. You saw my dad. He won't stop. This is my only chance."

I was starting to get desperate. He wasn't going to change his mind. He kept fingering the keys, itching to start up and get going.

"What about the hockey?" I said.

"What about it?"

"You promised me. I still haven't scored a goal."

"You will. Just keep practicing."

"Coach says we have a chance to make the play-offs. He's counting on you. He can't do it without you."

"Bull."

"It's true. We're all counting on you. Ruth, too."

"Her? What about?"

"She thinks you're going over to the rehab program with her. Remember?"

Buff squeezed the steering wheel and studied his knuckles without saying a word.

"You've made promises," I reminded him. "Obligations. You can't run away."

"I'm not running away! I'm getting myself straight!"

"Ruth says you can't do it alone, Buff. And she should know. She wants to help. So do I. Julie, too. We'll all help you. You can make it."

"Thanks but no thanks."

He was getting angry again. I was, too. I was losing my temper.

"Your father was right about one thing! You are a quitter!"

He grabbed me by the collar, ripping a button off my shirt, and pulled me to his nose.

"Take that back!"

He was thinking about hitting me.

"You are," I said.

He threw me away. My shoulder hit the door heavily. It hurt. Buff turned the key in the ignition, and the engine roared instantly. Then it settled into a steady rumble.

"Get out of my car," he said.

"No. And it's not your car. It's your father's car."

"I mean it. Get out. I've got to get going."

He was going to kick me out.

"I won't get out," I said. "You can't make me."

"Suit yourself," he said.

He got out, opened the garage door all the way, and got back in. He turned on the headlights, released the emergency brake, and revved the engine. Then he shifted into first and eased out the clutch. The car rolled forward smoothly, through the door and out into the night. He braked to a stop and looked at me.

"Close the door," he told me.

I wouldn't. Buff laughed and did it himself. The keys were dangling in the ignition. I could have grabbed them and tried to swallow them, but there was a big plastic tag on them. I would have choked to death. Buff got back into the car.

"You've got one more chance to change your mind," he said.

Crazy thoughts were flying through my mind. I had a French exam on Thursday. I was going to miss it. I hadn't said good-bye to Julie or my parents. And I didn't have any clean underwear.

"If we're going to go, then stop talking about it," I said.

Buff eased out the clutch and the car bumped over the snowy ground. He steered nicely out of the alleyway, braking at the road and looking both ways. When he put on the turn signal and looked past me to start the turn, he saw my face.

"If you're going to be depressed, you can't come," he said.

I was so tired, so worn down by everything, I couldn't help myself. I didn't even think about what I was saying. It just came out.

"Please don't go away," I said. "You've got to stay here. You said if I helped you out, you'd help me out. That's what friends are for, you said. I can't stop you from going to Canada, but damn it, don't you see what you're doing? It doesn't solve anything. And when your father finds out you've stolen the car, it'll be even worse. The cops'll be after you. And everybody who says you're no good, that you're too much trouble—they'll be right!"

Buff stared at me. Then he shifted into neutral and set the brake. I tried to calm down.

"You really would go to Canada with me?" he said.

I nodded.

"And you really would help me in the rehab program?"

I nodded again. "Ruth, too," I said. "She really likes you."

The engine idled throatily as we sat there. Buff was thinking. He turned on the heater when he saw I was shivering. The car warmed up immediately. Then he smiled at me.

"Maybe I should wait a couple of weeks," he said.

FIFTEEN

"Kill him! Kill him!" a fat woman kept screaming at me. She was rooting for Wilton. I'd just checked one of their players too enthusiastically and was skating to the penalty box for two minutes. If we won this game, we were in the play-offs.

Coach Anderson sent John Murphy and Buff out to help kill the penalty. They were playing well together. John Murphy had scored late in the first period on a pass from Buff. Now, halfway through the second period, we were tied with Wilton.

The noise level went up a couple of notches every time the referee dropped the puck. Crystal Rink was sold out. All 4355 seats were taken. I looked around from my seat in the penalty box. Art and Tina were sitting together way up near the roof. Making out under a blanket, no doubt. Ruth, Julie, and my parents were sitting together behind our bench. Every once in a while my mother glanced up at the ceiling, to check on the roofing tin. But it held. Just about everyone I knew was there, everyone except Mr. Saunders. Buff wouldn't even let him come to a practice.

Wilton had the man advantage. They kept trying to work the puck into our end. But John Murphy wouldn't let them. When he got hold of the puck, he lobbed it the length of the ice and half the crowd cheered—our half. Wilton had to skate all the way back to their end, get the puck, regroup, and start all over. That took time. The scoreboard clock ticked off the forty-five seconds remaining in my penalty. With ten seconds to go, Buff stole the puck.

He's done it a million times in practice. He skates toward you and then seems to give up, as though he's going to let you skate right by him or pass off. He starts to turn away from you, then all of a sudden he cuts back. His stick flicks out, he's got the puck, and he goes for your goal. All alone.

The goalie stopped the first shot, but Buff knocked in his own rebound. His arms shot up and the red light went on. Goal! The crowd went wild again. We were ahead, 2–1. When I got out of the penalty box, Coach Anderson waved me to the bench.

"Nice check," he yelled over the noise of the crowd. "I've never seen you so fired up before. But we need goals, not penalties."

I sat down. Buff skated to the bench and sat down next to me. People leaned over the wall to slap him on the back. But he didn't seem to notice. His eyes followed the play on the ice. He never took his eye off the puck, he was concentrating so hard. He'd been like this for a couple of weeks. Ever since the fight with his father.

"That was a nice goal," I said.

"I almost didn't get it," he said, not looking at me. "I should have fired three inches lower."

"Relax, relax. You did fine," I said.

Ruth told me the best thing I can do to help him is to support him. Not by babying him or lying to him but by encouraging him. By telling him he's OK. That's what Ruth is doing with him. He's staying at her house so they can talk about things. And all three of us are seeing a guy over at the hospital twice a week. Buff said that helps too. We're trying to get him to let his father come, too. But Buff says he isn't ready yet.

"Change 'em up! Change 'em up!" Coach yelled. "Third line!"

It was time for me to go out there again. I was getting tired.

"Tell Andy to look for you," Coach told me. I nodded. Just before the face-off, I told Andy that the right defenseman was leaving me wide open near the net. If he could get a pass to me, I'd bang it in.

Wilton was a good team. Most of their players were good skaters. But they didn't check much. Normally I didn't either, but this game was different. I decided to pick on somebody instead of having them pick on me. The right defenseman was bigger than I was, but he couldn't skate as well. So I checked him a lot. Maybe that's why he left me alone around the net. Anyway, Andy fed me a pass as we crossed the blue line. I skated a couple of steps with the puck and realized I was alone and running out of room. So I wound up to take a shot.

"Go for the four!" I told myself.

I took a shot that felt really good.

"Clang!" The puck hit the post! The goalie fell down and Wilton players fell all over him to smother the puck. The crowd cheered. When I sat down on the bench, Buff pounded me on the back.

"You almost did it!" he said.

"It was just like the targets!" I yelled back. I laughed. I was trembling all over. I could still feel the sting of the stick in my hands. It had been a hard shot. I had almost scored!

Thirty seconds later, Wilton got even. The crowd quieted down for the rest of the period. And when we went to the locker room at the end of the period, we were still tied. Everybody was screaming about how we were going to win, how we had to be tough. About how we were going to murder them, you know? Coach Anderson came in and paced back and forth, listening to us. His eyebrows were flapping up and down so hard I thought he was going to take off. Then he cleared his throat to speak.

"Listen up!" John Murphy said, banging his stick on a trash can to make everyone shut up. "Coach has something to say!"

Coach looked at us for a minute. His eyes

sweeping us like a searchlight. Then he spread his arms apart.

"We have one more period, gentlemen," he said. "One more period. I can appreciate your enthusiasm and confidence about the outcome of this game. You've worked hard all year. But let us keep this in perspective. No one will die of shame if we lose. No one will live ever after if we win. So what is the big deal?"

He closed his arms. Everyone started muttering about how right he was. Sweeney was standing next to him, using a tissue to mop up the blood where he picked at his zits. Coach frowned at us. And when Sweeney dropped the tissue and bent over to pick it up, Coach looked around at the team.

"I'll tell you what the big deal is!" Coach yelled. He booted Sweeney in the rear. "This is the most important game of your lives! Chicopee has a chance to make the play-offs! I want you to go out there and be animals! I want you to go out there and *win*!"

There was a lot of yelling and carrying on. People pounding each other and acting tough. I always feel a little silly doing it, myself. But this was a big moment for the Coach.

"Let's get 'em," John Murphy said.

"We're on our way over the top," someone else said.

And for a minute we made more noise than the crowd, hoping that Wilton would hear us and start shaking. Then we all charged out onto the ice. Everybody but Buff. So I hung back, waiting for him. He was sitting on the bench next to the locker, the way he had before. His hockey bag was unzipped and he was staring at it. I could see the upper half of a thermos.

The locker room at Crystal has rubber mats for floors. To protect your skate blades. So Buff didn't hear me. He thought he was alone, looking at the thermos and thinking. Then he decided. He reached out and I wanted to yell. Thank God I didn't. He zipped up the bag.

I backed out of the room and hustled to the bench. When Buff sat down, he was still thinking. There was a lull in the action as the crew patched a hole in the ice. I tightened my laces and listened to the crowd heat up. It would be a tough period.

"You know, I don't have to be like my dad," Buff said, out of the blue. "When he was a kid, all he ever thought about was hockey. That and winning. But I don't have to."

"No, you don't."

"My dad did, though. Hockey was the only way he could be somebody. But he's him and I'm me. And I don't want to be like him."

I nodded. We smiled at each other. And Buff looked much more relaxed, more self-confident.

"It was a good goal I scored," he said. "A real good one."

Then we smiled again at each other and Buff looked out on the ice to follow the play.

"Come on!" he yelled, slapping his stick against the boards. "Let's win this turkey!"

The ref dropped the puck and the third period started. The game was a cliff-hanger all the way to the end. But we lost it 3–2. I never did score my goal.

Coach Anderson was so pleased at the way we played he gave everyone a letter at the hockey banquet in May. Buff sat with me and my father. He won the Most Improved Player trophy. They gave it to him at the banquet. He'll probably be first string next year if he decides to play. He's not sure he will, but I hope he does. I still haven't scored that goal. Julie says she doesn't care. She likes me just the way I am. She's proud of me for being a good friend. Buff and I are clocking her at the AAU regional in two weeks. It should be fun.

All in all, we've been pretty lucky.